CW00970725

ENGLISH FICTION OF THE SECOND WORLD WAR

ENGLISH FICTION
OF THE SECOND WORLD WAR

Alan Munton

faber and faber

LONDON · BOSTON

For my parents

First published in 1989
by Faber and Faber Limited
3 Queen Square London WC1N 3AU

Photoset by Wilmaset, Birkenhead, Wirral
Printed in Great Britain by
Richard Clay Limited, Bungay, Suffolk

British Library
Cataloguing in Publication Data
is available

ISBN 0-571-14971-5

In an age when critical theory promises, or threatens, to 'cross over' into literature and to become its own object of study, there is a powerful case for reasserting the primacy of the literary text. These studies are intended in the first instance to provide substantial critical introductions to writers of major importance. Although each contributor inevitably writes from a considered critical position, it is not the aim of the series to impose a uniformity of theoretical approach. Each book will make use of biographical material and each will conclude with a select bibliography which will in all cases take note of the latest developments usefully relevant to the subject. Beyond that, however, contributors have been chosen for their critical abilities as well as for their familiarity with the subject of their choice.

Although the primary aim of the series is to focus attention on individual writers, there will be exceptions. And although the majority of writers or periods studied will be of the twentieth century, this is not intended to preclude other writers or periods. Above all, the series aims to return readers to a sharpened awareness of those texts without which there would be no criticism.

John Lucas

Contents

Acknowledgements

This is a virtually untouched subject, as far as criticism is concerned. I was therefore in particular need of good advice from those who read my drafts. I got it – from Paul Edwards, Ian Gordon, Richard Gravil, Cindy Hamilton and Nigel Mace. Michael Locke will remember numerous breakfast-time discussions in London. My colleagues in Plymouth worked harder so that I could enjoy a term free from teaching to begin this book. To Ronald Gray I am grateful for books, wartime memories and sound advice.

I gratefully acknowledge permission to use quotations granted by the following publishers, agents and individuals: Faber and Faber for *The Trap* by Dan Billany and *No Directions* by James Hanley; Macmillan for *The Home Front* by Arthur Marwick and *Eastern Approaches* by Fitzroy Maclean; Methuen London for *The Magic Army* by Leslie Mitchell, *Christopher and His Kind* by Christopher Isherwood and *Flesh Wounds* by David Holbrook; Longman for *The Cage* by Dan Billany and David Dowie; David Higham Associates for *Return via Dunkirk* by Gun Buster; Century Hutchinson for *Pebbles from My Skull* by Stuart Hood; Hodder and Stoughton for *The Fringes of Power* by John Colville; Charles Strachey and Elizabeth Al Qadhi for *Post D* by John Strachey; E P Thompson for *There is a Spirit in Europe . . .* by Frank Thompson; the Estate of the author and Chatto and Windus for *Caught* by Henry Green; George Weidenfeld and Nicolson for *Since the Fall* by Stuart Hood, *Under Siege* by Robert Hewison, *The Levant Triology* by Olivia Manning and *The Diaries of Evelyn Waugh*, edited by Michael Davie; Victor Gollancz for *Among You Taking Notes . . .* by Naomi Mitchison; Tessa Sayle for *Season in Purgatory* by Thomas Keneally; Sphere Books for *Nella Last's War* by Nella Last; Peters Fraser and Dunlop for *Put Out More Flags* and *The Sword of Honour Trilogy* by Evelyn Waugh, Peters Fraser and Dunlop and the author for *The People's War* by Angus Calder; Pan Books and Murray Pollinger for *Love, Sex and War* by John Costello; Harvey Unna and Stephen Durbridge Ltd and Jonathan Cape for *From the City, From the Plough* by Alexander Baron; the Estate of Elizabeth Bowen for *The Heat of the Day* by Elizabeth Bowen; Constable and the Estate of the late Patrick Hamilton for *Slaves of Solitude* by Patrick Hamilton. Quotations from *Daylight on Saturday* © J B Priestley 1943, and from *The Balkan Trilogy* by Olivia Manning © the Estate of Olivia Manning 1960, 1962, 1965, are reprinted by permission of William Heinemann Ltd. Quotations from *Valley of Bones* and *The Military Philosophers* by Anthony Powell are reprinted by permission of William Heinemann Ltd and David Higham Associates Ltd. Quotations from *Ride Out the Storm* © John Harris 1975 and *Dunkirk: The Necessary Myth* © Nicholas Harman 1980 are reprinted by permission of Curtis Brown Ltd, London.

Faber and Faber Ltd apologize for any errors or omissions in the above list and would be grateful to be notified of any corrections that should be incorporated in the next edition of this volume.

A. M.
January 1988

I
Introduction

' "Being alone don't count any more, nobody can be alone any more, see," ' says an ARP warden in James Hanley's Blitz novel *No Directions* (1943) as he insists upon rescuing a reluctant victim. War is a social activity. Men go out in groups to kill each other, and they die together. People being bombed in their homes or shot in the streets also die together. Out of such events there inevitably arise social changes with widespread effects. It is because people fight wars collectively that writers of war fiction must find ways of recreating collective experience, often undergone in situations of chaos whose meaning remains uncertain. The critic, following after, must find ways of ordering material so varied in content and so massive in quantity that at first sight it may appear unmanageable.

In this book – which is, as far as I know, the first lengthy study of Second World War fiction – I have confronted the chaos by using one main organizing category, the historians' term 'the People's War'. This defines the war as a specific kind of collective experience, whilst valuing that experience in ways that are consistent with the processes of valuing that take place in fiction. By limiting myself to this term, I hope to avoid letting the variety of war fiction tempt me into unnecessarily multiplying the categories for organizing it.

In making this limitation I have risked leaving out whole groups of novels and stories that particular readers may feel should have been included. This is unavoidable. I would prefer to establish a strong argument around a single concept, and allow later critics the opportunity to modify that argument and bring forward different organizing principles, than reproduce, in what is an introductory study, the multiplicity of possible means of organization that the fiction itself may suggest. There is one omission, indeed, that I particularly regret – there is no discussion here of novels concerning the war in the Far East. The lives of the expatriate British communities in Singapore and Shanghai were far from belonging to the People's War, but in differing so markedly from life in Britain, and in having their own ways of suffering, these lives make a significant comment upon the home front. J. G. Farrell's *The Singapore Grip* (1978) and J. G. Ballard's *Empire of the Sun* (1984) are the major novels of this experience.

In the following pages there are very few references to criticism written by others. This is partly because very little relevant criticism exists, partly because I have insufficient space to engage in critical debate. However, I must express my debt to Holger Klein's chapter on British war fiction in *The Second World War in Fiction* (1984). This is a survey of remarkable range which proposes all kinds of substantial relationships between works and categories of works. Klein identifies categories that I have no space to develop (the wartime thriller, for example), but his essay also suggested to me that it was not necessary to multiply categories in order to make sense of the material. Despite this difference of emphasis, several aspects of my discussion are influenced by his: we are in substantial agreement over Evelyn Waugh's *Sword of Honour* (1984) trilogy, for example. I have also been influenced by his view that war fiction is closely related to autobiography – to such an extent that on occasions I have, perhaps rashly, written as if war fiction and war autobiography differ very little from each other, a view that I believe is defensible in certain cases, particularly when the autobiography is written in a highly organized form.

Apart from the People's War concept, my primary theoretical interest is in narrative. For reasons that I explain in Chapter II, writers found themselves in a peculiarly difficult position when they attempted to write about the war while it was still going on. Specifically, they had difficulty conceiving endings. My discussion of this aspect of war fiction is necessarily influenced by Frank Kermode's *The Sense of an Ending* (1969). The question of endings is related to an author's view of the future, and since the People's War is a future-directed concept, my major theme and the problem of narrative meet in the recurrent discussions of narrative resolutions.

A further prominent theme of this book – though not an organizing principle – is the question of the representation of women in war fiction. The historical and anecdotal record shows that women's lives were changed in significant ways by the war, particularly in their work and in their personal lives. Yet war fiction scarcely recognizes these changes. In *Post D*, published in 1941 – a creditably early date – John Strachey wrote that 'Whoever else might fail to realise what they were fighting for, no women [*sic*] should have any doubt. The outcome of the war would decide whether women were to hold and extend their grasp on full citizenship in the modern world: or were to go back to the admitted dependence of former centuries' (Strachey, 1941, p. 23). The post-war fiction that I have characterized as 'epic' in Chapter IV is largely written out of a conviction that a woman's rightful position is a situation of dependence. I have tried to show the strategies by which these writers attempt to resist recognition of the freedoms that women established for themselves during the war. The strategies are consistent with those writers' resistance to the wider social changes made possible by the People's War. Beyond that, these writers – Waugh, Anthony Powell and Olivia Manning in particular – were projecting back upon the war years their own post-war disillusion and their own willing accommodations to the literary and political establishment.

This study also confronts another form of resistance: that of literary critics to the concept of 'war fiction'. The writing of 1939–45 has never achieved the status of the writing of 1914–18. I cannot here describe why that should be so, but it is worth remarking that as a *period* the Second World War has been refused critical recognition. In his essay 'Modernism, Antimodernism and Postmodernism', published in *Working With Structuralism* (1981), David Lodge sets out the conventional periodization for twentieth-century literature: first modernism (James Joyce and Virginia Woolf in the novel, but not Wyndham Lewis); then 'antimodernism', the more traditional fiction written by George Orwell, Christopher Isherwood, Graham Greene and Evelyn

Waugh during the 1930s. Then there is a jump to the post-war period and the 1950s of the Angry Young Men; the war is excluded, without explanation. In its literary aspect the war has disappeared into an Orwellian memory hole.

It is certainly the case that war fiction shares the attributes of 'antimodernism' in not being concerned with literary experiment or the troubled individual subject. The end of the modernist period in Britain was signalled when, in the late 1930s, Wyndham Lewis and Virginia Woolf chose to write novels about 'England' and about class, Lewis in his post-Munich novel *The Vulgar Streak* (1941), and Woolf in *Between the Acts* (1941). The war fiction written in wartime is not continuous with 'antimodernism', not least because no writers on Lodge's list (except Waugh) wrote well about the war, and because few writers on the Left wrote about the war at all: many were demoralized by it, as I shall show. The early 1940s produced a new, or newish, generation of writers: Henry Green and Patrick Hamilton at their best, J. B. Priestley finding himself as a propagandist, Alun Lewis at war, Dan Billany a new representative of the Left – most were unencumbered with the commitments and compromises of the 1930s.

The writing and publication of fiction in wartime faced two constraints: writers lacked time and publishers lacked paper. The figures on paper rationing and book production have been brought together by Robert Hewison in *Under Siege* (1977), his valuable study of the cultural life of London during the war years. These show that during the war there was a sharp fall in the quantity of fiction published. In 1939, 4,222 fiction titles appeared; by 1945 the number had fallen to 1,246. Paper rationing was a major contributory factor. At the outbreak of war publishers' paper supplies were limited to 60 per cent of the paper they had used between August 1938 and August 1939; by the end of 1941 this was reduced to 37.5 per cent, and the government repeatedly refused any increase.

Publication of new titles and reprints fell from 14,094 in 1939 to 6,747 in 1945. Publishers divided their paper ration among authors on the basis that enough copies be printed to cover the author's advance, with a small profit for themselves. Newspapers, reduced in size, had no space for extensive reviewing. The special conditions of war – the need to avoid boredom, in particular – meant that books sold out, often in a matter of days. *Now*, a literary journal carrying pacifist and anarchist writing, sold out all its wartime numbers, much to the pleasure of its editors. Expenditure on books rose from £9 million in 1939 to £23 million in 1945. Yet many books went out of print, and because publishers did not have to take risks, it was not necessary to promote new authors.

In these circumstances it was unlikely that any new school of writers would emerge. It is this, in addition to the physical difficulties of finding sufficient time to write that helps to explain why there is no 'major' war fiction of the war years and immediately afterwards. This I understand to be evidence that literary production is affected by the conditions under which it takes place, rather than evidence that writers became incapable. In any case it would be foolish to wish the war years other than they were. The situation as we find it, with all its strengths and imperfections, is what this book sets out to investigate.

II

Fiction and the People's War

The term 'the People's War' became current with the publication of Angus Calder's *The People's War: Britain 1939–1945* in 1969. Describing the effect of the war on civilian life Calder argues that the social structure of Britain was altered by the mobilization of resources needed to fight a war. During 1940–1 there existed amongst a significant proportion of the British people a dissatisfaction with the way the war was being run so deep as to generate political attitudes which were, or were very nearly, revolutionary in content. Two related questions were involved: the immediate question of the conduct of the war, and long-term considerations of the kind of society that should exist in Britain after it was won. There was a widespread belief that those who had fought (or, as civilians, had undergone) the war should benefit when it was over. General agreement existed that the way forward lay through planning; and since planning was associated with the Left, this carried with it the implication that there should be post-war socialist planning. This expectation was fulfilled to the extent that in 1945 the Labour Party won the first general election for ten years.

To compile information about the People's War, Calder drew upon the reports collected by Mass-Observation, whose observers recorded the behaviour and opinions of people throughout the country; others wrote diaries describing their own experiences. Because this material was gathered by untrained and only loosely co-ordinated individuals, its reliability as an historical source has been questioned. Calder defends his use of these materials as 'an indispensable aid to tracing popular views and reactions in all kinds of fields, from aerial bombardment to greyhound racing' (Calder, 1969, p. 13).

In a critical commentary upon the term, Arthur Marwick has

written that 'any snappy generalization such as "People's War" is open to all sorts of qualifications', for example that the war confirmed many traditional attitudes as well as encouraging new ones (Marwick, 1976, pp. 180–3). Marwick nevertheless finds four reasons for believing that the Second World War was genuinely a People's War:

> First, for a relatively short period during the blitz ordinary people were in the front line, bearing the direct brunt of enemy fire power; second, over the longer period of the whole war, direct participation in all aspects of the national effort by ordinary people was absolutely vital, first to survival, then to victory; third, the war for the first time gave a genuine influence to individuals who believed themselves to be spokesmen, not of the establishment, but of the people – film-makers like John Baxter and Thorold Dickinson, publicists like J. B. Priestley and Ritchie Calder . . .; and fourth, for all the powerful resistances that remained, there was in all sections of society a movement in favour of radical social reform. (p. 180)

This is a distinctly less political interpretation of the war than Angus Calder's, but it indicates that there is agreement among historians that 'the People's War' is a valid concept.

Literary critics are likely to feel that the detailed information on people's lives assembled in *The People's War* belongs unambiguously to their area of interest, for this is the kind of detail out of which fiction is made. Further, the level of generalization achieved by organizing this material under the heading of 'the People's War' is sufficiently secure to allow a critique of war fiction to be built around it.

From the outset it was recognized that the phrase 'a People's War' belonged to the Left. The most audacious use of the term during the war was by Tom Wintringham in *New Ways of War*, completed in June 1940 when invasion seemed imminent. Wintringham's emphasis is on 'the people's *war*', however, for his book contains instructions on how the civilian population should fight and defend itself. There are diagrams illustrating how to set up crossfire (these also appeared in the popular weekly magazine

Picture Post) and how to defend a house against attack, together with instructions for a home-made grenade that might stop a tank. Wintringham uses the classic argument for arming the people:

> A government of a country that has been long accustomed to peace is naturally reluctant to put explosives and lethal weapons in the hands of its citizens. A government that represents propertied classes is always terrified by the fear of revolution. If we are to have a People's Army we must break down this reluctance and this fear, and find for ourselves a government that will entrust to the people the means for their defence. (Wintringham, 1940, p. 85)

This passage, published in a Penguin Special, indicates the kind of thinking that took place after the retreat from Dunkirk. When Churchill told the House of Commons that the British would 'fight in the fields and in the streets', it is unlikely that he had in mind the kind of revolutionary transformation in the conduct of the war envisaged by Wintringham, but it is difficult to see how Churchill's hopes could have been fulfilled except on the basis of a people's army organized for its own defence. The political consequences of that would have been immense, and probably not to Churchill's liking.

Wintringham's experience fighting Franco's rebels in the Spanish Civil War with small, scarcely trained forces were his model for the defence of Britain. George Orwell had also fought in Spain, with the militia of POUM (Partido Obrero de Unificación Marxista), a highly political and democratized organization, and this experience encouraged him to believe that the Home Guard might become an organization with revolutionary potential. (The only fiction to take up these issues is Len Deighton's *SS–GB*, published in 1978, which is based on the premise that the German invasion succeeded early in 1941. The fighting during the invasion is conceived in conventional military terms, and popular resistance is shown as ineffectual to the point of being ridiculous. Deighton appears uninterested in the possibilities envisaged by Wintringham and Orwell.)

The reality of the People's War, in terms of injury and loss of life, was grim enough. It was non-combatant civilians who faced the first onslaught, not the fighting services. There were 22,428 civilian deaths due to war operations in 1940, and 22,350 in 1941, but only 3,884 in 1942; total civilian deaths due to the war were 63,689. Civilian casualties of this order are one aspect of 'total war', the complete mobilization of a country's resources for war. The army lost 144,079 killed between 1939 and 1945, the RAF 70,253.

One difficulty in using the term 'People's War' in a discussion of war fiction is that the concept is partly built up from that fiction itself. Calder quotes several times from Evelyn Waugh's novels and takes some particularly atmospheric passages from Elizabeth Bowen's *The Heat of the Day* (1949). In *A People's War* (1986), another valuable source based on Mass-Observation archive material, Peter Lewis structures his chapter on industry around the title of J. B. Priestley's aircraft-factory novel *Daylight on Saturday* (1943). This tendency is not sufficiently marked for the People's War concept to seem to chase its fictional tail, but it does suggest that fiction is not an autonomous activity separate from historical developments, and that under certain circumstances it can possess the same persuasive status as fact. This affects our understanding of the relationship between fiction and 'factual' autobiography, a question to which I shall return.

The relationship between fiction and fact is often an intriguing one. In his discussion of the internment of foreign nationals Calder mentions that some were detained in 'a derelict cotton factory infested by rats' (p. 152). This factory is evidently the setting for the internment camp in Alex Comfort's novel *No Such Liberty* (1941). The reason for this coincidence of interest is that both writers draw upon the same source, François Lafitte's *The Internment of Aliens*, a Penguin Special of 1940. Writers who are too young to have experienced the war as adults face a different problem of authentication. In Leslie Thomas's *The Magic Army* (1981) a middle-class girl exclaims, 'There are women going home with six or seven pounds a week in their pockets and they feel the war's the most wonderful thing that's ever happened'

(Thomas, p. 278). The figures are rather high, but this remark is a legitimate reinterpretation of Angus Calder's account of women's wartime earnings: 'There were undoubtedly a proportion of women who earned at male rates, even the occasional girl . . . who built up earnings at piece rates which exceeded those of many men.' In 1944, the year in which the novel is set, the average wage for men in metalwork and engineering was £7, for women £3 10s (Calder, p. 465), and it was possible for women to approach the male wage. In other words, Calder's *The People's War* has itself become a source for writers of fiction who want to ensure that their facts are accurate.

Leslie Thomas acknowledges his debt to this and to other books in a bibliography appended to the novel. The novel which acknowledges its sources is becoming increasingly common – Penelope Lively's *Moon Tiger* (1987) is another example – but J. G. Farrell's *The Singapore Grip* has a bibliography of nearly three pages. Len Deighton's *Bomber* (1970) and *Goodbye, Mickey Mouse* (1982) are among the most heavily researched of all war novels. This development makes it possible to distinguish between 'researched' and 'experienced' war fiction. The latter category usually includes work written during or just after the war that is a reworking of personal or communal experience. James Hanley's *No Directions* (1943), describing a night of the Blitz, is an example, as is Alexander Baron's *From the City, From the Plough* (1948) or Dan Billany and David Dowie's *The Cage* (1949). David Holbrook's *Flesh Wounds* (1966) is a later example.

'Experienced' or 'felt' novels possess a sense of immediacy that brings with it fictional authority. Novelists writing in later decades attempt to establish their authority by insisting that their fictions are authentic. Through research they attempt to establish for a new readership facts and attitudes that those who lived during the war took for granted. These research activities are inevitably conducted according to certain presuppositions about what was significant in wartime, so that the 'researched' novel does not so much reproduce the period as construct a post-war view of wartime life. In practice, researched war fictions very rarely possess the same atmosphere as works written during the war itself. Reviewers frequently praise post-war war fiction for showing life 'exactly as it was'. Since these fictions often differ widely among themselves in atmosphere, subject-matter and attitude – consider Leslie Thomas, Anthony Powell and Len Deighton, all of whom have been praised in these terms – it will be apparent that what the reader is being persuaded to accept as 'authenticity' is a very particular selective reconstruction from the available research materials. Each of these fictions is the product of a particular view of the war which the author wishes to promote under the protective cover of researched 'authenticity'.

In discussing war fiction I have situated each novel as participating in a debate around the concept of the People's War. It is not my intention to produce a definition of what the People's War may have been and then to measure the war fiction against the definition. A novelist's refusal to acknowledge the existence of the concept, or a decision to write in opposition to it (as Evelyn Waugh does) may be as significant as any endorsement. On the other hand, a novelist's wish to write in People's War terms can produce writing which does little to make the concept persuasive. The following example from Jack Lindsay's novel of the campaign in Crete shows such a failure:

Thinking of Sally – would she be on a day-shift now or cuddling up in her bed with the chintz curtains drawn, half-awake listening for the alarm-clock? Lured out at last by the thought of a cup of tea or a chat with Gladys? Or at the works kissing one of the shell-cases (as she said in her last letter), thinking how it might blow up the very German that was aiming at dear Ted? You never knew. (Lindsay, 1943, p. 80)

This is from *Beyond Terror: A Novel of the Battle of Crete*, which contains many examples of how not to write about the People's War.

Although the People's War concept can include a great deal of varied experience, it also acts as a limitation or boundary. Much that was commonplace in Europe and the Far East, notably occupation, did not occur in Britain. Alex Comfort, writing in 1948, assumes that the post-war novel will be concerned with Europe, with 'the first days of the Russian occupation of Berlin; the last days of the German occupation of Paris; Hitler and his doxy cremated in the ruins of the *Reichskanzlerei* among old petrol tins; the buffoons and charlatans of the peace conference . . .' (Comfort, 1948, p. 75). In practice, such subjects did not interest the writers of English fiction, and the question of how they might be realized never arose. English war fiction has evaded as many subjects as it has embraced.

The British mainland was neither occupied nor fought over. Britain's Jews – with the exception noted below – were not deported, as they were throughout Europe. There was no Resistance, and so no reprisals, as there were in every occupied European country. English villages and their inhabitants were not systematically destroyed as they were in the Soviet Union. Only the Channel Islands were occupied and – in an indication of what would have happened – its Jews, few in number, deported. 'Every country in this last war had its Fifth Column,' wrote Arthur Calder-Marshall in 1949; 'how large it was in Britain was never revealed because the country was never occupied' (*Our Time*, April 1949, p. 91). There were active collaborators and informers in the Channel Islands who caused the deaths and imprisonment of fellow islanders. Angus Calder believes that the population of Great Britain would have divided into resisters and collaborators, but that the Fifth Column would have been small: 'besides a no doubt tiny number of active Fifth Columnists, many reputable people, great and small, would have collaborated with the Nazis when the time came' (pp. 476 and 150). It is because that time did not come that there is no equivalent in English fiction to Vercors's occupation novel, *Le Silence de la mer* (1943), or the stories of the French Resistance, based on her own experience, in Marguerite Duras's *La Douleur* (1985, trans. 1986).

The only fictions to raise the question of collaboration and resistance in Britain are Len Deighton's *SS–GB* and Derek Robinson's *Kramer's War* (1977). The former has a police officer hero who moves from a form of 'legitimate' collaboration (criminal investigation: murderers must be caught, whatever the regime) to a form of resistance; but since German officers also participate in it for their own purposes, this is far from resembling the resistance movements that actually existed in Europe.

Despite the extent of suffering in Britain, particularly during the Blitz, British war experience was less severe than in Europe and distinctly less so than in the Soviet Union. The worst treatment suffered by British troops occurred in Burma and Malaya, particularly amongst those who were prisoners of war. It is perhaps significant that both popular memory, and fiction, have shied away from the Far East. The exceptions are J. G. Ballard's remarkable *Empire of the Sun* and J. G. Farrell's *The Singapore Grip*.

English war fiction did not have to confront such knowledge as Primo Levi had of the German concentration camps, but writers none the less had difficulty in finding an order for what they knew. The greatest problems arose amongst those writing about European resistance movements. For Stuart Hood, who spent a year with Italian partisans during 1943–4, ordering the experience has remained a permanent difficulty. He has used both fiction and autobiography (another indication of the closeness of those two forms). The novellas 'The Circle of the Minotaur' and 'The Fisherman's Daughter: a Tale' appeared under the title *The Circle of the Minotaur* in 1950. A novel, *Since the Fall*, followed in 1955. Set in the post-war years, it looks back to the period of partisan warfare. An autobiographical version of this experience appeared in 1963 as *Pebbles from My Skull*, and was reprinted in 1985 as *Carlino*, with a new Afterword showing how memory repeatedly undermines what the autobiographer believed to be the 'facts'.

If fiction deals with difficult experiences by situating them in a narrative 'out there' with an apparent logic of its own, autobiography admits that the experience is close to home, but suffers from the treacheries of memory, which unknown to the author works its own distortions, turning 'the truth' into something very little different from fiction. Again and again Hood discovers that his memory is at fault, yet the memory, not the reality, remains as truth for him. Fiction and autobiography merge and cross, two unreliable records which are for the reader varying truths rather than different genres.

Certain episodes in Hood's books occur in both forms. There is the occasion when a partisan group awaiting a parachute drop is joined by an additional man, who is immediately suspect. In *Since the Fall* Gavin Hamilton (a version of Hood) asks for him to be 'bumped off', a term in keeping with the comic-satiric tone of the book. In *Pebbles from My Skull* Stuart Hood, in his own person, tells his lieutenant: '*Bisogna che sparisca*' – he's got to disappear; and he does. It is not a question of which version is the more true, for each is true to the text in which it appears. It is rather a matter of how the truth is to be told, to what audience and for what end.

Just as people in Britain believed that never again should they suffer the social conditions of the 1920s and 1930s, so did the European Left believe that the post-war world should be transformed: for those who had actually suffered Fascism in Italy, France, Poland, Greece, Yugoslavia and the Balkan states, there was a far greater urgency than existed even in Britain. At Christmas 1943 Frank Thompson wrote from Cairo to his brother E. P. Thompson to describe what the possibilities for Europe might be:

> There is a spirit abroad in Europe which is finer and braver than anything that tired continent has known for centuries, and which cannot be withstood. You can, if you like, think of it in terms of politics, but it is broader and more generous than any dogma. It is the confident will of whole peoples, who have known the utmost humiliation and suffering and have triumphed over it, to build their own life once and for all. I like best to think of it as millions – literally millions – of people . . . completely masters of themselves, looking only forward, and liking what they see . . . There is a marvellous opportunity before us – and all that is required from Britain, America and the U.S.S.R. is imagination, help and sympathy. (Thompson, 1947, p. 169)

What, in fact, was the outcome? In *Since the Fall* Gavin reflects on what happened after the war:

'There was a moment when we seemed to be on the edge of something – as if everyone was going to become braver, wiser, more generous. Now there is nothing left but politics. Man makes his own best dreams impossible.' (p. 105)

During the war years it was felt all across Europe that a People's War was being fought. The post-war defeat of the parties of the Left, largely induced by the political settlements made by Britain and America at the end of the war, was a betrayal of the best dreams of the war years. The same defeat was suffered again in fiction. The success of Evelyn Waugh's *Unconditional Surrender* (1961) as the novel of partisan warfare is a success for pessimism and conservatism and for carelessness about people's hopes. Nevertheless, the sense that people had of looking forward 'and liking what they see' was extremely powerful, and in my discussion of war fiction I have made the sense of the future one of the tests of meaning.

A peculiarity of the literary history of the early part of the war period is the demoralization of the writers who had become well known during the 1930s. If any group seemed likely to thrive on a popular war, it was those writers who had built a reputation from their political radicalism, from their opposition to government measures against the poor at home, and who had supported the Spanish Republic during the Spanish Civil War. Yet this never became their war.

W. H. Auden and Christopher Isherwood, the two most prominent members of the 'Auden group', departed for the United States in January 1939, and caused a great deal of anger on the Left for doing so. War was inevitable, and they seemed to be ensuring their own safety. Isherwood's own description of their feelings during their journey shows that they felt the 1930s were over, that a break had occurred:

One morning, when they were walking on the deck, Christopher heard himself say: 'You know, it just doesn't mean anything to me any more – the Popular Front, the party line, the anti-fascist struggle. I suppose they're okay but something's wrong with me. I simply cannot swallow another mouthful'. To which Wystan answered: 'Neither can I.' (Isherwood, 1977, pp. 247–8)

Many people on the Left felt that with difficulty they had constructed a politics appropriate to their time that was disrupted by the outbreak of war, with all its immediate chaos and future uncertainty. Others tried to find a continuity in the chaos, but refused to recognize that anything new was occurring. Stephen Spender (another member of the Auden group) argued in a booklet entitled *Life and the Poet* (1942) that the suffering caused by the war was of no greater significance than the suffering that already existed in the world. He quotes the poet Geoffrey Grigson: 'The greatest intensities of suffering or evil are always being endured somewhere by somebody in peace or war' (Spender, 1942, p. 122). This is no doubt true, but it meant that the war did not have to be understood as a war; it was just another example of suffering. In this way the war was dissolved as a subject of particular interest.

Nevertheless, many writers did feel a need to understand the new period and to make sense of the war while it was still in progress. Their difficulties in doing so can be understood by looking at successive volumes of John Lehmann's magazines *Folios of New Writing* and *New Writing and Daylight*. Lehmann had been one of the outstanding editors of the 1930s, in effect creating the Auden group in the pages of *New Writing*. Its successor *Folios of New Writing* was published in 1940 and 1941, and in 1942 became *New Writing and Daylight*, published in book form once or twice a year throughout the war.

Folios of New Writing looked back to the 1930s – here are to be found Stephen Spender, Dylan Thomas, Rex Warner, Henry Green, George Orwell, Edward Upward, William Plomer and David Gascoyne. Only in an editorial to the Autumn 1941 number, entitled 'Looking Back and Forward', does Lehmann begin the long process of examining the effect of the war on contemporary literature.

He admits that the response of the best-known 1930s writers to the war had been puzzling and confused. These writers had been anti-Fascist when the government had tended to favour the Nazis and Italian Fascists, but now that they had to line up beside the appeasers they found it difficult to do so. They were suspicious of this change of allegiance by the men of Munich (who had tried to satisfy Hitler by betraying Czechoslovakia), wondering if the leopard really had changed its spots. It is not a strong argument to justify inaction: if they were anti-Fascist in the 1930s, why should they have doubts now, when Hitler's intentions were plain to see? Why should the Left be any the less vigorously anti-Hitler because the appeasers had recognized their own errors? Some, Lehmann said, remembered the enthusiasm that greeted the conflict of 1914–18, and the horror and disillusion with which it ended; these writers' admiration for the poetry of Sassoon and Wilfred Owen forced them to recognize the suffering of both sides, and fear of a similar development on this occasion inhibited their support for an anti-Hitler war. It required Churchill to come to power in 1940 before they resumed their activities.

Lehmann's third reason for the silence of the Left shows how strongly they felt the differences between the war years and the 1930s. These writers had anticipated a catastrophe which, despite their warnings, had not been avoided: with the outbreak of war a phase in their writing lives was over. Lehmann concludes: 'there remained, cargoes washed up on the shore from the wreck, some very beautiful verse and prose of permanent value' (p. 7). The 1930s writers had been unable to anticipate a wartime function for themselves; locked into opposition, they could not adjust to a People's War. This is all the more puzzling because the strong documentary element in the writing of the 1930s had prefigured the way things were to go: the very people investigated by Orwell in *The Road to Wigan Pier*, or by Mass-Observation, or who had been celebrated in hundreds of poems and articles, were to play a central part in the war itself. Why did writers not recognize this? Their hopes wrecked by the outbreak of the war they had so long anticipated, they fell at once into a demoralized silence.

That silence can partly be explained by the difficulties created for the Left – particularly the organized Left – by the German–

Soviet non-aggression pact of August 1939. This undermined the argument that the Soviet Union was the standard-bearer of opposition to Fascism in Europe, though it remained possible to say that Stalin was buying time to prepare his country against an inevitable German invasion. At the outbreak of war the Communist Party in Britain took the line that militarily this was an anti-Fascist war which should be conducted with vigour; when Douglas Springhall returned from Moscow on 24 September 1939 with the Communist International's declaration that it was an imperialist war in which the working classes could support neither side, there was confusion. In the 1930s the Communist Party had been central to the Left's idea of itself; even if one was not in the party, one nevertheless stood in a definable relationship to it. Changes of line by the Communist Party made it vulnerable to attack from a variety of positions that included the anti-Communist Left (George Orwell, for example), disillusioned fellow-travellers (the Left Book Club publisher Victor Gollancz), socialists and liberals, as well as the Right. The effect was to undermine self-confidence everywhere on the Left.

It was Rex Warner who made the most cogent case for utopia from within the war years themselves. In an essay entitled 'On Subsidising Literature' he summarized the various views of the future then current:

> All have in common the resolution that this time deeds not words are required, and that these deeds shall take the form of an organization of society that is both fair and efficient. In short it appears to be the wish of the vast majority of the people that after the war their Government should be, in some form or another, socialistic, and that the Government should, unlike those of the pre-war period, have a clear idea of what it is aiming at. (*Folios of New Writing*, Autumn 1941, p. 188)

This is a classic statement of the People's War position, and an early and prescient one. Warner goes on to say that the current vagueness in thinking about social and political matters was dangerous because it might lead in any direction, towards Fascism as much as towards socialism. He adds:

I should suggest that today this thinking about ends, about ideals, about suffering and happiness, about life and death is more needed than political and economic thinking. (p. 190)

This implies that the important thinking of the time should be conducted in and through fiction and poetry. Warner's stress upon thinking about ends is particularly relevant to a discussion of fiction and its relation to the future, and is a theme that I shall pursue here.

Several stories published by Lehmann show writers taking as their subject the very fact that they could not make sense of their present circumstances. One, Raymond Williams's 'This Time', is a satire upon those on the Left who believed that they could understand any political situation. A soldier, drunk or dreaming, recalls the pre-war confidence:

It was a good job they had seen through the illusions. If the war came they would understand it perfectly. And they understood themselves and the political struggle and the god fallacy. Munich, Danzig, Warsaw, Paris. 'This time we understand'. (*NWD*, Winter 1942–3, pp. 159–60)

A song runs through the soldier's thoughts:

Once before / We were unaware the chance we were waiting / Was close at hand. / This time we understand. (p. 159)

The break in the rhythm between the second and third lines disturbs his dreams:

It was a little frightening, the break of the rhythm. Remember how we laughed at anarchy and feared it? We are in it now. Where has the grand synthesis got to? What about the inevitable forces of history? Our movements are breaking up. Our masses scatter into thousands of frightened sheltering humans. War is tearing out our vitals . . . We are improvising, madly. Learning how to cook in fields, and make sanitary ditches. Starting from nothing, moving on to nothing again . . . It is anarchy, anarchy, anarchy. (p. 161)

Even the words of the Okey Pokey [*sic*] make an ironic comment on left-wing certainties: 'You do the Okey Pokey / And you turn about. / THAT'S WHAT IT'S ALL ABOUT!' The soldier finds he is nearly late for parade, where he 'turns about' with precision. But the wider meaning escapes him: he doesn't know what it's all about. In time of war fiction is forced to recognize its limitations as a means of interpretation.

In 1946 *New Writing and Daylight* published a symposium entitled 'The Future of Fiction'. Of the six contributors only one had anything substantial to say about the effect of the war on the writing of fiction. Rose Macaulay wrote that 'it has been a tragedy too vast, too gross, too ill-understood; it has clogged and stunned imagination, and intellectual activity has been paralysed' (*NWD*, 1946, p. 73). Of those young enough to fight she wrote:

> The communal living, the unsteady, chancey drug of danger, the constant keying up of nerve and sinew [*sic*], may have broken his mind into disorderly fragments, made consecutive thought, initiative and concentration difficult; if he writes he may write in spasms and fragments, without coherent pattern . . . Fragments, impressions, brief glimpses – these are, on the whole, the mode. (p. 73)

These remarks confirm the argument of this book, that those writing during the war were forced into constructing fragmentary texts which could not order or shape the experience of war on any significant scale. This is not a criticism of these writers, but a description of the consequences of the very real difficulties that they faced, and of their attempted solution to it.

The failure to understand these difficulties is partly responsible for the way war fiction has been treated critically. Since most of it was improvisation in the face of chaos, and is clearly not 'major', the period as a whole has been dismissed as having little significance. These are the 'lost years' of English fiction. Yet, quite obviously, a great deal happened. Everything depends upon how the years 1939–45 are defined. It is not unduly paradoxical to argue that they are significant precisely because indisputably great fiction was *not* written then. That absence is a measure of the impact public events can have upon the capacity to create. Creativity is not constant but vulnerable to difficult conditions. The authors who did go on writing during the war had to develop particular strategies in order to deal with the special nature of the period in which they were living. These strategies centre upon their conceptualization of the war as a period, and this question I shall now discuss.

Fiction written during the war was end-stopped by history. For the author, as a contriver of narrative, the climactic or concluding historical moment gave retrospective shape to a sequence of experiences which were otherwise difficult to order. The reader, reading forwards, anticipates or finds satisfying the resolution offered by a known historical moment; he may feel even more confidently situated in present time because his knowledge of the past – of how it 'worked out' – confirms his present experience of the narrative. For the author, working backwards, history can be a constraint. Unless the work is a fantasy, fictional events must be related to or must confirm actual occurrences known to the readership. This requirement reduces an author's freedom to choose the direction of a narrative, compared to the possibilities open to the writer of fiction not set in wartime. Some writers felt this constraint very heavily and abandoned the attempt to develop an unfolding narrative in favour of fragmentary structures that proceed without direction. To choose the form of the short story was also a means of avoiding the difficulties that followed upon not knowing the outcome of the war. 'Wartime' was a special kind of time; begun at a specific moment, it had – as everyone knew – to end, but the moment of its ending moved ahead of all anticipation, requiring a constant adjustment to the psychological space that still lay ahead. In these circumstances the most characteristic war fiction written during the war was short, limited in scope, intense in feeling, fragmentary in structure, and often climaxed or closed off by a known historical event.

Fiction about the war written after it was over has a quite different structure. Once the outcome is known the experience of the entire war is open to interpretation in ways not previously possible. Post-war fiction is most characteristically structured on a large scale. Writers often take the whole of the 1939–45 period as their subject, and write expansively. I have in mind the trilogies written by Anthony Powell, Evelyn Waugh, and Olivia Manning, together with the two war novels written by C. P. Snow. The scale often implies that the war can now be seen in epic terms; but heroic deeds, the usual subject of epic, do not in fact predominate. These fictions are often about disillusionment with the war, discovering in it futility or emptiness. Writers now find a moral confusion or contradiction that contrasts with the single-mindedness supposedly felt while the war was actually taking place. Freedom from the constraints of history has released these writers into self-criticism, the reflectiveness that follows upon action. These fictions are therefore inverted epics, in which the heroic temperament is undermined or the unheroic given privileged attention.

These novels were written by authors considered 'literary' rather than 'popular'. With the exception of C. P. Snow's war novels, and the first two volumes of Waugh's trilogy, this writing appeared, after long reflection, in the 1960s and subsequently. It had been preceded, in the 1950s, by an outpouring of popular works which vigorously asserted an heroic version of events, works which were heavily fictionalized in the double sense of being both in fictional form and palpably falsified. Most of these books are still well known: Paul Brickhill's *The Dam Busters* and *The Great Escape* (both 1951), Pierre Boulle's *Bridge on the River Kwai* (1952), *The White Rabbit* by Bruce Marshall (1952), *Cockleshell Heroes* by C. E. Lucas Phillips (1956), *Safer Than a Known Way* by Ian MacHorton (1958), and many others. A genuine heroic epic in fiction, Nicholas Monsarrat's *The Cruel Sea*, appeared in 1951. This onslaught made the heroic mode impossible for literary writers, who chose instead to write understated, ironic novels of wide scope about figures who fitted only awkwardly into the war, if they fitted at all. It is from this partially detached point of view that the post-war critique of the war years is made. By writing in trilogies or as part of longer novel sequences, the novelists I have named make a particular claim upon our attention. It is the claim to a particular authority: a claim to understand the war, of being able to grasp the whole of it and to situate it within the social and political history of our times. These writers use their authority, I shall argue, to present a socially conservative account of the war years which is at variance with what most people felt was actually occurring at the time.

To organize experience whilst in the middle of it is always difficult. It was doubly difficult to do so in the middle of unprecedented events: 'wartime conditions were such that writers found it difficult to establish a point of perspective from which to view what was happening around them' (Hewison, p. 97). The major technical question that arose was: how does one end a fiction? The writer has privileged access to those formal structures and conventions that allow fictions to be resolved, but where the outcome of a war is concerned, the novelist is no more privileged than the readership. A proleptic fiction guessing at the outcome of the war would be instantly disproved, and authors naturally did not attempt this. The answer had to be found by creating a space for fiction within the events of the war itself.

In these circumstances authors chose to limit their fictions to single incidents or to short periods of time. One night in the Blitz is the choice made in James Hanley's *No Directions*. Many writers used well-known historical events as motives, climaxes or endpoints in their fictions. For example, in Patrick Hamilton's *Hangover Square* (1941), George Bone commits a double murder as Chamberlain announces the declaration of war, and J. B. Priestley makes the second battle of El Alamein an inspiration for the factory workers in *Daylight on Saturday* (1943). The invasion of Crete is the subject of 'single-episode' fictions in James Aldridge's *The Sea Eagle* (1944) and Jack Lindsay's *Beyond Terror* (1943). In *There's No Home* (1951) Alexander Baron neatly solves the problem by describing an interlude in the war in Sicily, the month between arriving in Catania in August 1943 and moving on towards Italy in September. Such a strategy as this depends upon understanding the war as falling into identifiable periods.

The question of periodization is a difficult one. The years from 1939 to 1945 are, for the British, 'the war'. We mean many things when we use those words, but there exists a basic agreement as to what is meant in terms of shared experience, known facts, and extension in time. But for the Soviet Union the war ran from June 1941 to 1945, for the United States from December 1941 to the final date. For the French the war – considered as fighting between armies – was over by June 1940, and a period of occupation began, in which battle was replaced by passivity or by organized resistance. When people in these countries conceive the war years, the period known as 'the war' is thought of in an entirely different way than it is in Britain.

The years before are also different. The United States and the Soviet Union were onlookers during 1939–41, but in western Europe there was a continuity between the end of the Spanish Civil War early in 1939, and the fresh outbreak in September of that year. Such continuity is important, for the same weapons were to be used by the Germans against the British as the Germans had used against the Spanish Republicans (the 88mm anti-tank and anti-aircraft gun, and the Stuka dive-bomber). The question then was: could the British learn anything from the Spanish war? The military leadership thought not; but when the threat of invasion came in 1940–1, it was the recollection of guerrilla operations in Spain that provided Tom Wintringham and others with the model for a possible resistance in Britain. *Piece of Cake* (1983), Derek Robinson's novel about Hurricane fighter pilots, shows the importance of the Spanish experience – don't fly in formation, attack out of the sun, use back-armour in seats. Only by learning the lessons of Spain in the weeks before the Battle of Britain were they able to survive the assault itself.

There were also contemporary periodizations, ways in which those living within the years 1939–45 tried to understand the experience they were undergoing. Churchill was a shrewd periodizer, and many people came to understand the war in terms that he proposed for them. After the success at El Alamein in November 1942 he urged caution: 'Now this is not the end. It is not even the beginning of the end. But it is, perhaps, the end of the beginning' (Calder, pp. 351–2). Orwell too had a strong sense of period. He wrote a diary (unpublished) running from 10 July to 3

September 1939, his end-date suggesting that he saw the declaration of war as a final post-Munich episode rather than the beginning of something new. His next diary, from May 1940 to August 1941, was concluded because he believed that 'the quasi-revolutionary period which began with Dunkirk is finished' (Orwell, 1970b, p. 463). He begins again in March 1942 with Cripps in India and the threat of a separate peace between the Soviet Union and Germany. He ends on 15 November with a report of the church bells ringing for El Alamein, making the same choice of ending as Churchill. To periodize the war requires the political interpretation of an historical moment that is not yet complete.

There was also a form of non-historical short-term periodization. Civilians threatened by bombing or by the V1 and V2 rockets that fell in 1944–5 had to find a way of dealing with the possibility that their deaths might (or might not) occur, knowing that if they were killed it was not a matter they could do anything about. This created in many people the hedonist option of living from day to day. The 'period' was made as short as possible, so that the claim to have survived could be made again and again. Another version of short-term periodization is recorded by Naomi Mitchison in her diary. 'Jack and Helen are really frightened,' she wrote of her brother J. B. S. Haldane and his future wife, Helen Spurway, 'Helen saying how earlier it has been periodicity that got her – would she ever wash her hair again . . . I wonder how many people are scared like that' (Mitchison, 1986, p. 302). The fear that one may never again carry out a commonplace action may be a mild neurosis in peacetime, but in war it is a not unreasonable attempt to give order to a difficult situation. In a massive democratization of fear every threatened person could conceive his or her own life as a narrative, not quite completed. Everyone becomes a potential subject for fiction.

Periodization became more difficult after the end of 1942, when for the British the war ceased to be a matter of spectacular defeats or victories and became a hard and persistent struggle. The long slog through Sicily and Italy from July 1943 to May 1945 is the outstanding example of an undifferentiated period, ending only with the conclusion of the war. It is because the year 1943 lacks major events to which fiction can be attached, that novels dealing with that year face difficulties. Maureen Duffy's skilful overview of the war, *Change* (1987), is strongly periodized ('So ended the period of our innocence', p. 63) around well-known episodes: but 1943, represented by the end of the North African campaign and the beginning of the invasion of Italy, is indistinct, so that D-Day in June 1944 is reached sooner than the pace of the novel leads the reader to expect. The tendency to periodize weakens when the future begins to open out more hopefully. Conversely, the difficulty of ending a novel set in 1943 is shown by Patrick Hamilton's *The Slaves of Solitude*, which was begun during the war and laid aside, completed in 1945–6 and published in 1947. The lonely but sympathetically ordinary Miss Roach is offered an unexpected night at Claridge's in the last days of 1943:

> Then Miss Roach, knowing nothing of the future, knowing nothing of the February blitz [of 1944] about to descend on London, knowing nothing of flying bombs, knowing nothing of rockets, of Normandy, of Arnhem, of the Ardennes bulge, of Berlin, of the Atom Bomb, knowing nothing and caring very little, got into her bath and lingered in it a long while. (pp. 241–2)

Up to this point Hamilton has avoided specific historical references, partly because little 'happened' in 1943. Put into difficulties by the time that has elapsed between the events described and the date of publication, he is forced to historicize radically in order to situate the reader in relation to his ending. In passing, Hamilton mentions the atomic bomb, which ended (it is argued) the war against Japan, but which has now become, in its subsequent development, a possible ending of a particularly conclusive kind for the contemporary reader.

After 1943, fiction might be attached to D-Day or VE Day (8 May 1945). There are many novels of the battle for Normandy, few of the end of the war. Normandy is represented in my discussion by Alexander Baron's *From the City, From the Plough* and by David Holbrook's *Flesh Wounds*. These Normandy fictions bring in another factor, the possibility of a changed future. For Baron, success in Normandy is not a conclusion; it is part of a continuity that reaches forward not only 'across the map, towards Germany', in the novel's final words (Baron, 1979, p. 191), but towards a future in which the possibilities created by victory may transform the post-war world, or be betrayed by it.

From the City, From the Plough is a novel of collective experience, describing men of all ranks from private to colonel. The commonest narrative strategy for such fictions is to build up sympathy for a number of characters and engage the reader's feelings by allowing some, but not all, to die; the selection is usually made on moral grounds. Baron's novel is exceptional in that no named person survives. Men of the Wessex Regiment, already exhausted, have been asked to ambush German guns so that American tanks can proceed:

> Among the rubble, beneath the smoking ruins, the dead of the Fifth Battalion sprawled around the guns which they had silenced; dusty, crumpled and utterly without dignity; a pair of boots protruding from a roadside ditch; a body blackened and bent like a chicken burnt in the stove; a face pressed into the dirt; a hand reaching up out of a mass of brick and timbers; a rump thrust ludicrously towards the sky. The living lay among them, speechless, exhausted, beyond grief or triumph, drawing at broken cigarettes and watching with sunken eyes the tanks go by. (p. 190)

There is hope in this indignity. If certain men had been allowed to survive, their characters would have spoken too clearly about Baron's beliefs and intentions. By reducing them to anonymity he ensures that the reader must reflect upon what this collective dying means. We are to understand that it is a commitment to the possibilities of the future.

When a novel follows this strategy, it places itself in a definite relationship with the future that it envisages. One period – that of the novel itself – is projected forwards so that another may be conceived. This future, not present in the novel itself, becomes another possible period. When the author suggests that the suffering and destruction actually shown in the novel are a preparation for better things, people's lives can be thought of as open to transformation. This is proposed at the end of Holbrook's *Flesh Wounds*.

Every war novelist stands in a particularly acute relationship with the past and with the future because in the act of writing he or she is forced to clear a space within a period already heavily defined by other means, particularly by readers' knowledge of history. The marked periodization of war fiction is consequently one of its distinctive features. It is noticeable that almost every war novelist takes care to establish as soon as possible the date and place of events. The novelist writing during wartime dare not risk working within too wide a span in time; novelists writing after the war is over have the advantage of knowing the temporal limits of 'the war', but are at the same time constrained by knowing that every reader has an idea of the war years against which his own fiction must struggle in order to define itself. It is because history asserts itself so powerfully within war fiction that in the present discussion I have placed a strong emphasis upon the precise time and place in which events occurred. When the subject is war, history imposes itself as much upon the critic as upon the novelist.

In reading war fiction we shall find that work is a recurrent theme. War transformed the conditions of work for almost everyone. Men and women could be conscripted into the armed forces and their auxiliaries, or into factories. It was Ernest Bevin, Minister of Labour from 1940 to 1945, using sweeping powers under the Emergency Powers (Defence) Act of 1939, who directed labour at home, causing at the same time some of the most far-reaching social changes of the century. A significant decision was made in December 1941, when unmarried women between the ages of twenty and thirty were called up and given a choice between entering the auxiliary services (ATS, WAAF, WRNS) or taking jobs in industry. 'By 1943', writes Angus Calder, 'it was almost impossible for a woman under forty to avoid war work unless she had heavy family responsibilities or was looking after a war worker billeted on her' (p. 383). Women were categorized as 'immobile' or 'mobile'; the latter, young and unmarried, were moved around the British Isles as the ministry required.

Conscription for the armed services began in May 1939 – too late, many thought – and on 4 September all men between eighteen and forty-one became liable. The army grew from 400,000 in May to 1,128,000 in December. Reserved occupations – which included journalists but not authors – were excluded from conscription, depending on age. At the outbreak of war there were also 400,000 men in the Territorial Army and the same number of full-timers in Civil Defence, with over a million part-timers in addition. The Auxiliary Fire Service, whose members massively outnumbered the regulars, became unpopular with the public (no fires) and with the regulars, whose conditions of work they undermined (Calder, pp. 58–60, 78).

War fiction gives human substance to these changes. Henry Green's *Caught* (1943) shows the tensions between the AFS and the regulars, whilst John Strachey's lightly fictionalized *Post D* (1941) describes the work of an ARP warden. In the factories it was soon apparent that conscripted or 'diluted' female workers could do skilled work as well, and often better, than the men they replaced. The consequent difficulties are well described in J. B. Priestley's *Daylight on Saturday*, set in an aircraft factory. In the services there was an obvious distinction between 'hostilities only' recruits and experienced regulars, and this is a frequent theme in the fiction. Nevertheless, during five years of war, conscripts became experienced soldiers themselves. It is arguable that by the end of the war Britain was fighting with a people's army. This is how Dan Billany describes them in his novel *The Trap* (1950):

Here there were, trudging through the rain [on an exercise], bricklayers, dustmen, teachers, 'bus-conductors, plumbers, ploughboys, engineers, riveters, painters, bank-clerks, journalists, butchers – fathers, sons and brothers: middle-aged men down to boys like Shaw: their personal lives abandoned in scattered corners of the country. (Billany, 1986, p. 104)

Those personal lives were abandoned in order to learn a new job, to find a new if temporary role in one of the services. That was the predominant experience of the war years: of being trained into a new competence.

At home, most people experienced the war as deeply tiring. 'In offices, factories, ministries, shops, kitchens the hot yellow sands of each afternoon ran out slowly; fatigue was the one reality', wrote Elizabeth Bowen in *The Heat of the Day* (p. 86). The diary of John Colville, who was a Foreign Office civil servant, then Churchill's Private Secretary, and later a fighter pilot, shows how rapidly work was transformed, even before Churchill took power. On 11 September 1939 Colville arrived at the Foreign Office at 11 a.m.; in October a 9.30 a.m. start at Downing Street is 'disgustingly early', but on 26 January 1940 he is 'almost blind with overwork' (Colville, 1985, pp. 21, 43, 84). Naomi Mitchison records that on VE Day 'all but the very young looked very tired when they stopped actually smiling' (Mitchison, 1986, p. 321).

Although much extra work fell to men, who might have part-time ARP or firefighting work in addition to their regular jobs, it was women who took the full weight of the changed circumstances. This becomes apparent in one of the most remarkable of wartime diaries, that written by Nella Last for Mass-Observation. She was a working-class woman living in the shipbuilding town of Barrow-in-Furness. By September 1942 she was running a home, and a Red Cross shop, worked at the Women's Voluntary Service centre on Tuesdays and Thursdays, and at the WVS canteen on Friday afternoons. These energetic activities were carried through at considerable cost to herself in nervous stress. This is what could lie behind 'cheerfulness':

> I wonder if it's true that all women are born actors. I wonder what I'm *really* like. I know I'm often tired, beaten and afraid, yet someone at the canteen said I radiated confidence . . . I've a jester's licence at the Centre, and if I stick my bottom lip out and mutter, 'Cor lummy, you've got a blinking nerve' like [film comedian] Gordon Harker, I can often do more – no, *always*

do more – than if I said icily, 'I think that was a perfectly uncalled for remark, and I'd like an apology'. What would I *really* be like if all my nonsense and pretence was taken from me? I have a sneaking feeling I'd be a very scared, ageing woman, with pitifully little. It's an odd thing to reflect: *no* one knows *any*one else, we don't even know ourselves very well (10 September 1942). (Last, 1983, p. 217)

I know of no war fiction which recognizes women's subjectivity as existing in the way described here. Nella Last's feelings are both subversive and tragic. There was a considerable propaganda investment in working-class cheerfulness; to reveal that it was *acting* would have undermined one of the main strategies used to integrate the working class into the war effort.

Nella Last must define herself by means of a shared popular culture, imitating a comedian to achieve male respect where she works. To herself, however, she scarcely exists at all. This passage shows her being defined by others, or by a popular culture that can be appropriated for her to play her part. Such a crisis ought to be the content of war fiction, making accessible the otherwise withheld experience of women. Narrative fiction would privilege and legitimize events and feelings which as diary entries are soon overwhelmed by the banal chaos of passing time. Such fictions have not been written, perhaps because realistic writing lacks the technical resources to engage with difficult mental states. Modernism, always ready to welcome the disturbed subject, had broken up by 1939. Virginia Woolf's *Between the Acts* (1941) is built around a village pageant celebrating English life; with war imminent, history must be recovered and 'Englishness' again defined. Woolf treats with irony materials that wartime propaganda was to take all too seriously, but it is at this point that the modernist subject disappears, re-emerging only in the post-war work of Samuel Beckett.

It is nevertheless possible for a reader to construct a narrative out of the diffuse materials of a diary. Nella Last can be shown redefining herself. 'A growing contempt for man in general creeps over me . . . I'm beginning to see that I'm a really clever woman in my own line, and not the "odd" or "uneducated" woman that I've had dinned into me' (1 August 1943, p. 255). 'I looked at his [her husband's] placid, blank face and marvelled at the way he had managed so to dominate me for all our married life, at how, to avoid hurting him, I had tried to keep him in a good mood, when a smacked head would have been the best treatment' (10 May 1945, p. 282). It was work, in the new circumstances caused by war, outside the home and in daily contact with other women, that gave Mrs Last this confidence.

She was undoubtedly exceptional, and it needs to be said that working for the WVS was somewhat different from working in an aircraft factory. For women in industry, working away from the home for the first time, the war years were a moment of decisive liberation from pre-war moral and social restrictions. There was a sense of worthwhile collective activity at work, and of new opportunities away from it. Nevertheless, most industrial work was repetitive and boring, whether done by men or by women. Women proved their competence, but were as likely to find work alienating, in Marx's sense, as did men. *War Factory*, a Mass-Observation study published in 1943, showed this. Alienated work implies the existence, somewhere, of fulfilling work, and for this possibility to be raised without being realized was deeply frustrating.

For men in the army there were two kinds of work: fighting and labouring. Fighting was by far the least important. 'I had the normal skills in killing', remarks Stuart Hood (Hood, 1963, pp. 12–13). Killing was the skilled aspect of army work. The majority of the army were working-class men who spent most of their time as labourers. As a former gunner puts it, army work was 'marching and drilling, constant cleaning of guns and vehicles, digging latrines, waste-pits, trenches, gun-pits and dug-outs, cooking meals, waiting on officers; a soldier's military training and skills are used periodically but work and boredom predominate' (Ronald Gray, letter to the author). Most war fiction ignores work and boredom, but there are some remarkable pages in Dan Billany's *The Trap* describing exhaustion from digging trenches into the rock of the Libyan desert. The outstanding record of work, and what soldiers felt about it, is found in Spike Milligan's war memoirs, for example the description of digging a Command Post given in *Mussolini: His Part in My Downfall* (1980, pp. 126–30).

A short story by Graham Greene, 'Men at Work' (1940) does isolate killing as work. The activities of a committee at the Ministry of Information, where nothing of any value is done, is contrasted with the German bombers on a daylight raid over London. The condensation trails 'showed where men were going home after work' (Greene, 1977, p. 68). But this recognition of war as work is most uncommon.

Unfortunately for the status of war fiction, novels about work have rarely entered the canon of received texts. Work exists as a subject in Dickens and Hardy, in Gissing and in Robert Tressell's *Ragged-Trousered Philanthropists*, and during the 1930s there had been a number of novels about mining, by Harold Heslop and others. Critical orthodoxy has marginalized this kind of writing so that the self-realizations arising from work have never been as important as the questions of manners and morals generated by women's response to male desire. For an author to take up the subject of immature young men living in a single-sex society is immediately to be at a disadvantage. Fiction describing the business of killing, and all its associated activities, must struggle to achieve the authority already granted to the novel of morals and manners. Killing is, after all, only work.

III
Stories of War

An account of novels written about the war while it was still in progress will necessarily reproduce the sense of uncertainty felt by the writers themselves. The attempt to impose an order on wartime chaos required an unusually self-conscious approach to the question of structure, but writers found such varying solutions to the problem that it is not possible to find a consistent pattern. It is possible, however, to draw attention to the strategies pursued in their fictions by authors caught in a difficult situation. To isolate an ordering principle is to identify something of the terms in which the author conceived the war: narrative speaks through what it evades as much as by what it pursues. The question of periodization, with its implications, will therefore consistently arise. It is somewhat easier to situate these novels in relation to the People's War theme, or to discuss their attitudes towards work – including war as work – and to the problem of finding a role in the war, as well as to expectations of the post-war years.

The pre-Dunkirk attitude can be seen in Nevil Shute's *Landfall* (1940), a novel of the 'Bore War' period, written before 'the people' had become a force in the revised conception of British life. Shute takes an unembarrassed view of the superiority of the middle class over the working class. Flight-Lieutenant Jerry Chambers (not a fortunate conjunction of names) marries Mona, who works in a snack bar and says such things as 'you didn't ought to do that'. To make herself into a suitable wife she takes lessons to improve her speech, something that Jerry approves because he himself 'had deeper roots in England than she had' (Shute, 1962, p. 240). That remark belongs to the conservative attitudes of the 1930s, part of an outlook that many believed would be overthrown by the new populism of the People's War. By November 1940 Mass-Observation was reporting that 'in the last few months it has been hard to find, even among women, many who do not unconsciously regard this war as in some way revolutionary or radical' (quoted in Calder, p. 160). From this moment onwards popular and serious fiction alike would have to find ways of acknowledging the importance of 'the people'.

There were other issues from the 1930s still to be resolved, however. In *Put Out More Flags* (1942), another 'Bore War' novel and one of the few genuinely funny books about the war, Evelyn Waugh finds comedy in the chaos caused by the evacuation of working-class families into the genteel world of the English countryside. Basil Seal collects bribes by threatening to billet the appalling Connolly children on his well-off neighbours: that is the only role he can find. Basil belongs to the 1920s. He is one of that 'race of ghosts . . . no longer contemporary in sympathy' as Waugh himself describes the novel's characters.

But there are more serious themes in this novel than a little bribery. By examining the new wartime life through the eyes of an older generation, Waugh is using a well-established satirical technique to distance himself from what he is mocking. The social irrelevance of these people provides exactly the detachment he needs. They also provide his theme: what roles can Basil Seal and Ambrose Silk find in this war? The answers are not only more serious but also more troubling than we might expect from this predominantly comic novel.

Waugh deploys his outdated cast of characters in full awareness of the likely objections to them: that is part of the comic effect. At this date the objections would come from the Left, or so Waugh pretends to believe, setting up his provocations to draw into the open the stereotyped set of responses that for him make up 'Left politics'. A game is being played, in which the author attributes certain beliefs to the reader, and then outrages them. Of Alastair Digby-Vane-Trumpington we are told:

> During the General Strike he had driven about the poorer quarters of London in a closed van to break up seditious meetings and had clubbed several unoffending citizens. (p. 45)

Who believes these meetings to be 'seditious' – Waugh, a narrator, or Alastair? If Waugh, is he being serious? If a narrator, does he have the author's approval? 'Unoffending' suggests Alastair was engaged in random violence. The provocative indeterminacy of Waugh's satire ends, for Alastair, when he decides to take 'a modest but vigorous part' (Waugh, 1942, p. 45) in the war; he is the first of this 'race of ghosts' to do so. To find a role is to become immune from satire; to be unemployed, like Basil, is to remain the object of satire:

> In the new, busy, secretive, chaotic world which developed during the first days of the war, Basil for the first time in his life felt himself at a disadvantage. It was like being in Latin America at a time of upheaval, and, instead of being an Englishman, being oneself a Latin American. (p. 49)

Latin America was for Waugh a model of the politically objectionable, so it is not surprising that it should stand against 'Englishness' to define Basil's exclusion. In 1939 Waugh had published *Robbery Under Law*, based on his visit to Mexico in 1938. This is one of the truly corrupt books of the 1930s, for the journey was paid for by a son of Lord Cowdray with the intention that Waugh should write a defence of Western-owned oil companies – Cowdray's Mexican Eagle among them – which had been expropriated, to the delight of the Mexicans, in 1938. Waugh's book was to be part of the oil companies' propaganda campaign. He obliged, opening with a personal statement of conservative political belief, and ending with an attack on the Spanish Republic, which fell to Franco a few months before the book was published in June 1939. It is through nationality, Waugh says, that communities develop local loyalties, but 'not in terms of race' (Waugh, 1939, p. 17); Franco fought for unifying national traditions 'to prevent Spain becoming like Central America' (p. 269), that is, broken up by socialism and internationalism.

Put Out More Flags should be read as the successor to this book, rather than to the novel *Scoop* (1938). According to Christopher Sykes, Waugh could not find employment in the war for many months, perhaps because his right-wing political views – his 1936 interview with Mussolini, the pro-Italian convictions of *Waugh in Abyssinia* (1936) – were known and distrusted. In the novel, Waugh's problem is dramatized as Basil Seal's, who finally joins the Commandos (so did Waugh). This redeems him from his earlier comic misdemeanours as billeting officer, and he is accepted into the war.

Ambrose Silk is differently treated. He is a homosexual whose pre-war love for a Brownshirt, Hans, he describes in an apparently pro-Nazi story, giving Basil the opportunity to remove Ambrose to Ireland just ahead of arrest. Once there, he must move on: 'the dark, nomadic strain in his blood, the long heritage of wandering and speculation allowed him no rest. Instead of Atlantic breakers he saw the camels swaying their heads . . .' (p. 219). It is the usually irresponsible Basil who makes a serious cultural and political point when Ambrose argues that Hitler is a figure of fun, as Chinese scholars took the military man to be. Basil asks (it is 1940) whether these scholars minded invasion. ' "Not a hoot, my dear, not a *tinker's* hoot" ', replies Ambrose. ' "And you're starting a paper to encourage this sort of scholarship" ', says Basil ominously (p. 177). Ambrose Silk is shown as a Jew without a nation, and as a 'yellow nineties' homosexual and aesthete without loyalty to Britain. Waugh's nationalism is, after all, expressed in terms of race.

The ending found for Basil says that the outcast can be redeemed by discovering in himself the need to fight. It is after Dunkirk, when ' "There's only one serious occupation for a chap now, that's killing Germans" ' (p. 221). Here, and in Sir Joseph Mainwaring's belief that there is a new spirit abroad in Britain ('poor booby, he was bang right', p. 222), Waugh wishes to be heard saying that despite his politics he too wants a place in this war. Yet in the ending found for Ambrose Silk the worst of that politics reasserts itself to say that there is no place in the defence of Britain for a homosexual Jew with internationalist cultural sympathies. As we shall see in Chapter IV, Waugh's view of who should fight the war, and on what terms, recurs as a major theme of the *Sword of Honour* trilogy.

*

The defeat of the British Expeditionary Force (BEF) in Belgium and France in May 1940 was followed by the retreat towards Dunkirk and the evacuation of Allied troops to England. Skilful propaganda turned this disaster into a triumph. Denigration of the French became official policy. The British press was told that 'It is now no secret that on several fronts, the French failed to withstand the assault . . . In fairness to the British Army, and its commanders, it cannot be too highly emphasised that it is the Allied High Command that has been outmanoeuvred and the armies of the French that have been outfought – not the BEF' (Harman, 1980, p. 243). Anti-French attitudes occur not only in the autobiographies and fiction of Dunkirk, but in fiction dealing with later episodes in the war, such as H. E. Bates's pseudo-Resistance novel *Fair Stood the Wind for France* (1944). The two related works I shall discuss here are Gun Buster's autobiographical *Return via Dunkirk* (which went through several editions after first publication in 1940, and was reprinted in 1975), and John Harris's novel *Ride Out the Storm* (1975).

Surveying war writing in 1941 Tom Harrisson described *Return via Dunkirk* as 'a straight account of an artillery unit retreating from the Germans, absorbing in its graphic detail' (Harrisson, 1941, p. 416). Far from being straightforward, this book inaugurates the strategies subsequently used in most accounts of Dunkirk: diminish the significance of the military defeat, confuse what happened during the rearguard action around Dunkirk, denigrate the French contribution, and define the final evacuation as heroic.

Gun Buster's battery covers the retreat and the rearguard, going into action as the main forces depart. This deflects attention from the retreat itself and gives the impression that there was continued positive action against the Germans. The choice of a rearguard battery as a subject becomes particularly significant at Dunkirk itself. Gun Buster's Y-Battery is the last BEF battery to come out of action, on the evening of 1 June; it had been part of the perimeter defence that allowed the evacuation to take place until that time. This emphasis conceals the fact that it was the French forces who formed the true rearguard, allowing the BEF to be taken off until 11.30 p.m. on 2 June. On 3 and 4 June over ten thousand French troops, including most of the rearguard, found themselves abandoned. It was a betrayal.

This account of the story of Dunkirk is consistent with official policy. Gun Buster shows the French as having no discipline in retreat and as repeatedly trying to push the British off the road: 'a crowd of panic-stricken French poilus were trying to drive their lorries in the darkness right through our marching infantry . . . Angry words passed . . . We were just in the mood to shoot if necessary' (p. 242). British convoys tried to push through in exactly the same way, as Anthony Rhodes shows in a distinctly less propagandist account of the retreat, *Sword of Bone* (1942). For Gun Buster French looters are thieves, but British looting is treated with tolerant amusement. The blonde daughters of a French farmer, who look like 'typical Saxon Gretchens' (p. 162), are assumed, on no evidence whatever, to be Fifth Columnists. The French are worse than unreliable, they are a threat.

It is in Gun Buster's skilful use of first-person narrative to create a persona appropriate to the crisis that this book most resembles fiction. The narrator is portrayed as amused, sensitive but disciplined, inwardly calm but perturbed when it is right to be so. He speaks, somehow, for everyone in the battery: 'we', 'us' and 'our' abound, yet the reader may observe that he is a captain who speaks almost exclusively to other officers; sergeants scarcely appear, private soldiers not at all. *Return via Dunkirk* marks the last point when it was possible to conceive the war without the people who were to fight it. It was after Dunkirk that the People's War can be said to have begun.

Although attitudes soon changed, precisely because of the ineptitude shown in Belgium and France, the propaganda books did not disappear. They took on a new life decades later as sources for novelists attempting to ensure the accuracy of their own fictions. John Harris acknowledges his debt to Gun Buster in a note to *Ride Out the Storm*. This allows him to claim that his novel is securely based on fact. The effect of such research is to reproduce unchanged the propaganda attitudes of a specific moment without allowing for subsequent changes in wartime attitudes, or for revisions made by later historical research. John

Harris repeats Gun Buster's worries about the existence of Fifth Columnists, and reduplicates his anti-French attitudes: when a rescued man arrives on the deck of a destroyer among a group of Frenchmen he is told: 'You don't want to be with a lot of French bastards. Come and have a cup of tea' (Harris, 1976, p. 192).

Harris transforms Gun Buster's blandness into officer-Britishness, as these parallel passages show:

> 'Make two piles of the stuff on the bed', I said to my servant. 'A little pile of what we can take, and a big pile of what we can't' (Gun Buster, p. 196).

> 'Got my batman to make two piles, one of the stuff I could take, and one of the stuff I couldn't. Then we threw 'em both away' (Harris, p. 160).

Both writers attempt to demonstrate the British officer's natural capacity for survival. In doing so both ignore the defeated soldiers' capacity for anger at their defeat. This was intense, but is denied expression. Gun Buster speaks for his men because they could not be trusted to speak for themselves. In Harris's novel the anger is replaced by a less politically damaging emotion – shame: 'The attitude of the other ranks seemed to be . . . one of shame that they'd been beaten but full of certainty that it wasn't their fault' (p. 119). It was, we are invited to believe, the fault of the French; for indiscipline and chaos 'had started with the French and spread to the B.E.F'. (p. 120).

Such novels as *Ride Out the Storm* are not directed towards any future except 'ultimate victory', triumph without social or political content. The purpose of such writing is to show the supposed British virtues of endurance, determination and cheerfulness in adversity. To achieve this the author must make the historical moment authentic while at the same time insulating that moment as fully as possible from any analysis that might generate criticism of the propagandist view that is being promoted. Dunkirk marks the last occasion when the British class structure was largely intact and could try to fight a war without fully involving the British people. By contrast, such a moment as the Normandy landings of

1944 implies a break with the past and the imminence of a transformed future. For these reasons novelists of conservative outlook prefer moments of national crisis, such as Dunkirk, to moments of national triumph, such as Normandy.

No Directions was published in 1943, and is a characteristic wartime novel in that it is short and limited in scope; its time-span is a few hours before and during a bombing raid on London. It is untypical of war fiction in being about an artist. It is also untypical in at first defining the Blitz as an apocalyptic moment, but subsequently refusing to allow the narrative to be dominated by that concept. Apocalypse is overcome by the force of narrative, which insists upon its own persistence. When there are survivors to tell the story, the apocalyptic is reduced to the simply destructive.

The novel describes a group of people living in a four-storey house in Chelsea, with a basement shelter. In the house, Richard Jones, an ARP warden, attempts to persuade the house's occupants into the basement when a raid begins. Old Mr and Mrs Frazer insist on making cups of tea first; Mr and Mrs Robinson do not come because the husband is tuned to a broadcast from Bolivia. A sailor immobilizes Jones by holding his nose for a considerable time. The comedy continues when Clem Stevens, an artist, and his wife Lena set out from the top floor with a huge uncompleted canvas. Jones is exasperated: ' "But why in heaven they will *bring – that – bloody – tearing – thing* everywhere they go I don't know" ' (Hanley, 1943, p. 89). They are not as absurd as he thinks, for the artist and his wife are 'carrying a world between them' (p. 119) that is significant for everybody. The flat-dwellers eventually gather in the basement. A bomb falls close by; Johns, the sailor visiting the house, is killed, the rest survive.

The reader is likely to be hard worked to distinguish among the novel's main characters – ten in 147 pages – whilst engaged with Hanley's prose, which is concentrated and demanding. Hanley's people have no sense of what direction their lives might take, or what meaning the war may have for them. They are foolish and inadequate, but what they feel matters. Mr Robinson asks himself

the crucial question of the People's War, and receives an answer
that must often have been given:

'D'you ever ask yourself where all this is going to end, where it's
all leading to, you know, how it'll end sort of thing. Do you,
ducksie?'
    'Afraid I don't dear. I just think – well, I'm breathing, and
that's something.'
    'Um!' (p. 133)

Clem, the artist, has a better sense of possible endings. His
painting, possibly entitled 'Daylight', is an attempt to give meaning to the war by envisaging it as moving towards some hopeful
ending; but like everyone else he is caught in the middle of things.
Lena, his wife, half-explains to the warden why Clem will not let
go of it: ' "There's a reason, but you wouldn't understand – yet" '
(p. 117). The picture is incomplete, the war is as yet unfinished,
and the two must be completed together. Meanwhile the canvas,
shoved behind dustbins in the basement shelter, is the disregarded
talisman that ensures that a future for these people is still
imagined, even though they cannot conceive it for themselves, and
find the canvas itself only a nuisance.

While their future is imagined, these awkward and dislikeable
people are, unknown to themselves, protected by the Thames, 'a
girdling strength, round streets and buildings, round walls, round
people, children, round those working, those asleep' (p. 62). In its
care for the future and its sympathy for those under stress, this is a
People's War novel, but it is untypical in making no claim that
these people are a community.

It is in such passages as Lena's vision of the protecting curve of
the Thames, or the elderly Mrs Frazer slowly putting one foot
before another as she goes downstairs, that the meaning of the
novel lies. Such meaning is not apocalyptic. The novel tends
towards an apocalyptic moment, but sheers away from it. Clem,
high on a building, feels an intense upward pressure from the earth
as iron, steel and stone come to life around him: 'Wood and stone
and steel alive with wrecking power.' He seems to welcome the

destruction and to thank God for it: ' "God!" he said, "it's magnificent, it's – " ' (p. 140). Then he sees something white moving below and hurries down to it:

> He reached out his hand, something seemed to explode under it. A mad beast threshing, he knew it was a beast, he felt electric waves running across its back. He grabbed at the head, he caught hold on a leather, he was jerked into the air, the beast dragged him after it, they were in the street, they were in the middle of this down-rushing sea . . . And then against the light he saw it real. A big white stallion loose, a maddened animal, he held on, he could not let go his hold on this. (p. 141)

Eventually the horse calms down and follows, 'huge shy and shambling' (p. 142). The artist has mastered a natural force, and this is his true purpose, not to welcome destruction.

Apocalypse is a moment of violence in which God avenges those who have suffered, and history is brought to an end. To posit the end of history causes the future to vanish. No narrative can proceed without some future in view. Novels concerned with spectacularly destructive moments such as the Blitz always find strategies to defer or evade the apocalyptic. In *No Directions* this occurs when Clem catches the white horse. Because the beast symbolizes a positive force, perhaps England itself, certainly something valued among the destruction, narrative persists by telling of new events and making from them new meanings.

The refusal of home-front war fiction to be tempted by the apocalyptic possibilities of bombing is a measure of its commitment to collective experience. History does not come to an end. There must be a future, however diminished by loss. In Henry Green's *Caught*, another novel about the destruction of London by fire, we shall find a particularly ingenious instance of the evasion of apocalyptic temptations.

In a prefatory note to *Caught*, Henry Green writes that it is 'about the Auxiliary Fire Service which saved London in her night blitzes'. This implies that the Auxiliaries made a more important contribution to fighting fires at that time than did the London Fire

Brigade. In the novel, 'Regulars' are shown as no better – and sometimes worse – than Auxiliaries when the bombs begin to fall on 7 September 1940. A successful role has been found and its importance is polemically asserted in this novel.

Caught is a special kind of narrative. The novel was begun in June 1940, when the firemen had done nothing; its climax in the Blitz lay in wait for the author. The novelist obviously faces difficulties when an ending is known, or strongly suspected, from the outset. Green's solution is particularly skilful. The novel begins 'out of time', rather as certain pieces of music do, before a rhythm is established. The narrative eventually moves forward, but with the utmost reluctance. Green creates a narrative equivalent of the 'phoney war', moving out of empty time into the significant events of history. Elusiveness is a characteristic of all Green's fiction; he resists allowing his subject to be 'placed'. To be so caught by history is what the significant experience of the novel must avoid, and its narrative strategies are consequently designed as a set of evasions. Above all, the Blitz itself must be both experienced and prevented from achieving overwhelming significance as an apocalyptic moment which values or places everything around it.

The wish to avoid being caught in history is related to another purpose. This is a novel about men and action, in which women are troublemakers. Richard Roe, the central figure, tells the story of the Auxiliaries' first night of firefighting to his sister-in-law; but he ends with an aggressive outburst at her: ' "God damn you," he shouted, releasing everything, "you get on my bloody nerves, all you bloody women with all your talk" ' (Green, 1943, p. 196). Roe is ashamed of what he has said, but this attack also marks the moment of his release from the pressure of the historical moment: 'He felt a fool at once and, in spite of it, that he had got away at last' (p. 196). How is this escape achieved, and why is it done through an attack on a woman?

Caught begins in November 1939. Richard Roe, a widower and an Auxiliary Fireman, is visiting his son Christopher, aged five, who some months earlier had been abducted from a store by a woman who turns out to be the sister of his Fireman Instructor,

Arthur Pye. This first section of the novel does not inaugurate a continuous sequence in time. The abduction episode is told through Roe's memories both of the event itself, his later inquisitive visit to the store, and his son's actual experience of it, given by an omniscient narrator in parenthetical paragraphs. The result is a complex mix of memory and present-tense narration, designed to make the reader uncertain when the immediate events of the novel are taking place. The narration then moves backwards and forwards across Roe's experience before and after the outbreak of war. Gradually this uncertain chronology hardens into the record of known historical events.

We are now about to watch the mental breakdown of Pye. This occurs within history. As the Blitz nears, historical events are recorded with increasing persistence: Norway (April 1940), the invasion of Holland and Belgium (May), Dunkirk (late May). By April 1940, 'too disturbed to notice the invasion of Norway', Pye becomes convinced that many years before he had had sexual intercourse with his sister, failing to recognize her. He returns in memory to the years before the First World War; as the anticipated climax approaches, the incidental stories with which the novel is dotted occur further in the past, as if what is to come cannot be faced. The climax of Pye's increasing insanity occurs during the evacuation of Dunkirk (26 May–4 June). Pye, who is in charge of the sub-station, goes for a walk in the moonlight, returning later with a snotty-nosed boy of eight. 'Each man . . . was aghast at the news [that Pye is missing], for the evacuation of Dunkirk was on. In that deadly moonlight brothers were dying fast, and not so far off. A week's time and it might be anybody's turn' (p. 165). Pye is found out by a superior officer. At this point the narration jumps to Roe's story of the Blitz, and only on the novel's last page do we learn the full story: that Pye, faced with disciplinary action, gassed himself before the bombing began.

When the climactic moment comes, Green uses a startling narrative device. The Blitz is not given in the expected narrative sequence. The reader is told that 'some months later, after nine weeks of air raids on London, Roe was unlucky one morning. A bomb came too close' (p. 172). Convalescing, he tells the story of his experiences to Dy, his sister-in-law. This device prevents the Blitz functioning as an apocalyptic moment climaxing the novel. Narrative must persist beyond such events, its survival evidence of the human capacity to overcome and control extreme experiences.

Green ingeniously splits this Blitz story between Roe's awkwardly told version, and a parenthetical omniscient narration written in vivid literary prose. In the following passage, the reader sees the first efforts of these amateur firemen from within (admitting mistakes) and from without (showing the scene as beautiful). Roe is speaking:

> 'And green as we were, you don't know how good some of us were that night, Regular and Auxiliary. Shiner was superb. He should have been in charge of our pump. Because I made a Piper mistake almost at once. You see there was no room left to put our suctions down into the water. As soon as that first wave of bombers passed hundreds of men came out of the ground, it was surprising really, and went back through the mounds of burned-out stuff to get back to the fire. There wasn't room to get in among their pumps at the dockside.'
>
> (Nearby all had been pink, the small, coughing men had black and rosy faces. The puddles were hot, and rainbow coloured with oil. A barge, overloaded with planks, drifted in flames across the black, green, then mushroom-skin river water under an upthrusting mountain of fox-dyed smoke that pushed up towards the green pulsing fringe of heaven.) (pp. 181–2)

The combined effect of the two points of view, one in close-up, the other as spectacle, is to charge the scene with emotion. Roe's inability to explain clearly what has happened to him has the sadness of a great moment not told; if experience is made valid by being turned into stories, Roe has failed. By contrast, the long perspective of the parenthesis dignifies these men, but we cannot suppress our knowledge of the confusion we know is occurring within the fire. However, the reader is also required to accept that the firemen's heroism depends upon their now being 'real men', their masculinity validated: ' "There we suddenly were, men again, or for the first time" ', Roe says (p. 191). Green's Auxiliaries create a moment in the People's War when ordinary people become remarkable. Then comes Roe's outburst at Dy, already quoted. Women, who talk too much, cannot understand how male power constitutes itself in action. In this version of it, the People's War turns out to be solely a man's war. Roe escapes from being 'caught' in the historical moment by his assertion, against his sister-in-law, of the timeless value of male solidarity.

J. B. Priestley's *Daylight on Saturday: A Novel About An Aircraft Factory* is self-consciously a People's War novel. Priestley celebrates the post-Dunkirk period through a representative group of men and women working in an aircraft factory. It is a novel of collective experience in which a narrative with multiple strands is resolved by the impact of a major event in the war. Three-quarters of the novel covers four days in October 1942, dramatizing the argument that because the war is stagnating, morale in the factory is low and production declining. But this is the week before El Alamein. The narrative jumps to the day of the Eighth Army's breakthrough against Rommel: 'This was no ordinary Monday, though as yet nobody in the factory was aware of the fact' (Priestley, 1943, p. 231). By midweek the tide has turned in the factory just as it has in the desert and everybody is working harder.

James Cheviot, the general manager, believes that in this war 'you come in the end to people and to what they think and feel and are frightened of and hope for ' (p. 304). The novel was conceived and written after November 1942, by which time the elements of the People's War outlook had been assembled. The novel is consequently able to assert with confidence the value of 'the people' in the war effort: 'Where these factories are, there is power'. They will remain power-houses in the post-war period: 'What we don't know yet is for whose sake their power will be operated. We can only hope' (p. 3). A couple marry in the expectation that their children will be brought up in 'a world of socialism and engineering' (p. 302).

Here works Arthur Cleeton, the foreman who is 'ready to work until he dropped (and indeed had come close to doing it in the summer of 1940) . . . because he really believed in liberty and democracy' (p. 25). Here is the works supervisor Bob Elrick who worked so hard after Dunkirk that his exhaustion looked like drunkenness. He is a Nietzschean superman: 'Probably the secret of his despair, his dark impatience and sudden fury, was that having fought with Titans on the heights he could no longer live carefully on the lower slopes' (p. 85). The Soviet Union is popular among all the workers, as the visiting Tory peer Lord Brixen discovers – when he mentions the Red Army's victory at Stalingrad 'the applause was huge and almost instantaneous' (p. 254). The novel ends with James Cheviot committing himself to the future interests of working people as (after the morning shift) they come flooding out of the factory into the Saturday daylight.

Priestley makes the conditions of work a class issue between those in management who understand 'the human factor', and those who think only in terms of machines and organization. This is dramatized in the contest between the 'deeply undemocratic' upper-middle-class manager Blandford and the works superintendent Bob Elrick, who is working class, impulsive, rude, drinks too much, and assaults a young woman worker. Nevertheless he is presented as essentially right in his attitude to hard work, and Priestley is clearly committed to him. However, his energy is not required in the post-war years, for he is crushed rescuing a woman worker thrown into a machine by an insane man who thinks it requires a sacrificial victim.

Despite his democratic attitudes, Priestley makes some significant distinctions between men and women workers. He implies that 'diluted' female labour is less important than male labour: men and boys get closer attention in training than girls and women. The accounts of women are often patronizing: 'a comfortable little woman with no brains at all'; 'a dreary young woman'; 'she was a pathetic little object with stringy hair' – all these remarks are made with the narrator's authority. Men are not spoken of in the same way. By contrast, 'Don't go thinking there's a lot *in* men, dear, 'cos there isn't. That's why they're a nice rest after being with women' is a remark usefully recorded, but Elrick, falling for the girl he later sexually assaults, feels 'the alien but wonderful presence of Woman herself, the unfathomable feminine idea', whilst Mrs Cleeton lives in 'the feminine world of impulses, intuitions, presentiments, and premonitions' (pp. 35, 108, 275). This clutter of understanding, idealization and contempt for women does not read very well beside the novel's People's War claims; Priestley, writing when outspokenness often took the form of being outspoken against women, is endorsing values and attitudes that were – and often still are – prevalent in the British Labour movement.

Priestley also sexualizes the work experience of the permanent women workers, represented by Gwen Ockley. Before the war she had taken a job in an engineering shop 'to do a man's work among men so that she could lead a sensible, hard, independent life, and cut the feminine nonsense right out'. Aware of the implications of this, Priestley carefully explains: 'She was not really the completely mannish type, not like a few freaks she had met' (p. 18). She succeeds in her work so that the men 'more or less' treat her as one of themselves. Her ability – which is insisted upon – is offset twice: first by the suggestion of lesbianism, conceived as butch: 'seems to try an' look like a lad', a woman remarks (p. 293); second, by her falling hopelessly in love with Elrick and marrying unsuccessfully to forget him. As Elrick lies dying he recognizes that she has always loved him. The price that a woman pays for competence in work is a sexually grounded criticism firmly endorsed by the narrative.

Daylight on Saturday can hardly be called a successful novel, but it is the one novel of the war years that makes an explicit claim to define the People's War and to value it. This was consistent with Priestley's other public activities, notably the 'Postscript' broadcasts which he made for the BBC between June and October 1940. These established him as a spokesman for 'the people' and 'the community', a function he pursued in this novel and in *Three Men in New Suits* (1945). Priestley was very much 'in the war', and his commitment to its transforming possibilities was the most public of any made by a wartime novelist.

*

Many people worried about whether or not they were 'in the war'. To be out of the war was widely regarded as a deplorable condition, one that had to be overcome.

Almost without exception, war novels celebrate action of some kind, showing how varying competencies in new roles contribute to the central purpose, 'the war effort'. No doubt plenty of people were happy enough to get out of the war if they could (there was an exodus of the better-off to the Lake District, for example); and perhaps there existed a third category: those by temperament incapable of taking any interest at all in the war. This group is represented in fiction by Miss Enid Roach, the thirty-nine-year-old publisher's reader living in conditions of permanent social embarrassment in the boarding-house of misfits described by Patrick Hamilton in *The Slaves of Solitude* (1947). Miss Roach is afraid of the war. Watching a newsreel she experiences 'fear of life, of herself, of Mr Thwaites, of the times and things into which she had been born' (p. 27). She is right to fear Mr Thwaites, whose cruel loquaciousness enables him to tyrannize over her and the other boarding-house inmates, and she comes to fear her friend Vicki Kugelmann, a German woman of thirty-eight who comes to the boarding-house and takes Mr Thwaites in hand, with consequences that explode the entire neurotic community. The fourth actor in this obscure drama is an American, Lieutenant Pike, who hopes to start a laundry business in Wilkes Barre, Pennsylvania, and who offers marriage to every woman he meets, including Miss Roach. These people are barely competent to conduct their own lives, let alone contribute to anything so demanding as the war effort.

The Slaves of Solitude is in many ways the antithesis of the war novel. It takes place during the month of December 1943, when nothing of military significance occurred except the sinking of the *Scharnhorst* on Boxing Day – but on that day the boarders are shown to be preoccupied by their own drama of drunken impropriety. Written largely from Miss Roach's point of view, the novel foregrounds her ostrich indifference: 'If you could do nothing to alleviate a situation, what sense was there in thinking about it, talking about it, taking any interest in it?' (p. 164). Although this

attitude is not endorsed by the author, it does allow him to show
how this point of view can be held, and makes it possible to be
ironic towards some characteristic activities of the People's War.
Obsessive listening to the radio news is done here in a 'test match
spirit' (p. 165), whilst Miss Roach is unable to interpret the sign
'NO CIGARETTES. SORRY' as evidence for an understand-
able difficulty in supply, but as an insult to herself, 'a sarcastic,
nasty, rude "sorry" ' (p. 100). Her ignorance makes this a war of
neurotically troubling deprivations, a pilfering war,

> sneaking cigarettes from the tobacconists, sweets from the
> confectioners, paper, pens and envelopes from the stationers,
> fittings from the hardware stores . . . The war, which had
> begun by making dramatic and drastic demands, which had
> held up the public in style like a highwayman, had now
> developed into a petty pilferer, incessantly pilfering. (p. 101)

To show neither cheerfulness in adversity nor any understanding
of the simple mechanics of war is a mild subversion of more usual
attitudes, but to be no more than annoyed by the war guarantees
one's exclusion from it. In this way Miss Roach makes herself
insignificant.

Patrick Hamilton specializes in finding meaning in the insignificant. The boarding-house (still known, from its former function,
as the Rosamund Tea Rooms) is situated in Thames Lockdon
(Henley-on-Thames), and to the outsider the occupants appear to
suffer 'a condition of dullness, torpidity, inactivity, stupidity, and
silence' that is barely credible; but through 'this apparent mortu-
ary of desire and passion' there run waves of 'hellish revulsion and
unquenchable hatred!' (pp. 157, 158). These waves emanate
initially from elderly Mr Thwaites, who adopts a stylized language of his own, using such phrases as 'I Hay ma Doots', 'Verily'
or 'in Troth' as a strategy to dominate others, forcing them to
interpret him on his own terms. He affects to believe that Miss
Roach has a particular liking for the Russians, making her suffer
for their successes, which will eventually somehow make everyone 'equal': ' "The Coalman, no doubt, will see fit to give com-
mands to the King," he said' (p. 18). Eventually Mr Thwaites's

verbal and psychic aggression goes too far, and his suggestion that Miss Roach is having an affair with a youth of seventeen to whom she has been kindly, brings the novel towards its climax:

> With the realisation of his implication, with the memory of her walks with the Poulton boy, of their innocence and simplicity, of the glad, sad, maternal feelings which she had felt towards the boy as he had unfolded his ambitions, with the idea of gossip of such a kind having arisen in regard to such a relationship, Miss Roach lost control. The filth of the suggestion seemed like filth reeling round in her own head and blinding her. (p. 200)

She pushes Mr Thwaites, who falls. The next day – is it her fault or not? – he dies of peritonitis, muttering, 'Yea, Verily' to the end. Hamilton, a moralist, makes it plain that a little cruelty has gone out of the world.

Miss Roach's other oppressor is Vicki Kugelmann, a German long resident in England, who also possesses a language of her own, in this case the dated slang of the 1920s ('vamping', 'mud in your eye', 'be sporty, old thing') which she uses to oppress the inhibited Miss Roach, whom she calls, with cruel intent, 'the English Miss' and 'Miss Prim' (p. 127) when they are involved in an inconclusive struggle over the American lieutenant. It is Vicki who sees Miss Roach with the Poulton boy and conceives the notion of an affair between them.

Like the lieutenant, Vicki is described as 'inconsequent' (p. 86), a significant criticism in Hamilton's moral scheme. It is after Mr Thwaites's death that we are shown what Hamilton believes is morally consequent. Mr Prest, a hitherto enigmatic presence at the Rosamund Tea Rooms, turns out to be a retired pantomime and vaudeville performer, who is called back to the stage because younger actors have gone to war. Miss Roach goes to see him as the Wicked Uncle in *Babes in the Wood*, where the man the boarding-house thought 'common' is a triumph with the children. He comes off stage with, perhaps, tears in his eyes:

> There was an extraordinary look of purification about the man – a suggestion of reciprocal purification – as if he had just at

that moment with his humour purified the excited children, and they, all as one, had purified him.

And, observing the purification of Mr Prest, Miss Roach herself felt purified. (p. 233)

Up to this point Hamilton has recorded the minute details of social inhibition and the subtle destructiveness of private languages; here, in the public gestures and collective language of the theatre, with its capacity for creating laughter and pleasure, the oppressive world of the Rosamund Tea Rooms is blown away. The complex structures of suffering are replaced by the simple goodness that arises from wishing to please others.

There is much that has required purification. Hamilton's characters may be morally inconsequent, but their habitual cruelty makes them significant. Mr Thwaites is a secret admirer of Hitler: hence his fear of Russian success. Vicki Kugelmann's personal cruelty can be interpreted as having a political meaning, one that Miss Roach cautiously provides, timidly hoping that she is wrong. The recurrence of this theme – that cruelty and political attitude are related – suggests that she may be correct, and that Hamilton means us to recognize the politics latent in individual unpleasantness.

Were not all the odours of Vicki's spirit – her slyness, her insensitiveness – the heaviness, ugliness, coarseness, and finally cruelty of her mind – were not all these the spiritual odours which had prevailed in Germany since 1933, and still prevailed? (p. 133)

Despite Miss Roach's distress – these thoughts occur after she has been called 'the English Miss' – and her excessive conclusions ('was not Vicki a Nazi through and through?'), we are intended, I think, to understand that there is some truth in these reflections. Collective cruelty is made possible by cruel individuals. By placing Vicki in the Rosamund Tea Rooms, Hamilton infiltrates into a characteristic English institution an example of the state of mind that the British were fighting. It is in this sense that *The Slaves of Solitude* is a war novel. Unknown to herself, Miss Roach's struggle with Vicki puts her briefly 'in the war', rather than out of it. She remains essentially fearful and indifferent, however, and deeply in need of the concluding invocation: 'God help us, God help all of us, every one, all of us' (p. 242).

The Slaves of Solitude is a comic novel of manners with a moral conclusion and an understated but pervasive politics. Into the novel's circumscribed arena come English, German and American lives, displaced and distressed by a war whose existence they hardly recognize but which creates the conditions which expose their weaknesses and wickedness, redeeming only Miss Roach and Mr Prest. The novel is political on its own exacting terms, and does not need to speak the language of the People's War to be the outstanding novel of non-combatant experience.

Dan Billany's *The Trap*, and *The Cage*, written jointly by Billany and David Dowie, are central to my argument concerning the special structure of texts written in wartime. Both books were written in Italian prison camps in 1943. 'The cage' is the name given to the seventy square yards of wired enclosure in which 150 British officers were held at Capua, near Naples. The title of *The Trap* alludes to the immediate fact of imprisonment, but has – as we shall see – far wider implications.

Dan Billany, a lieutenant with the 4th Battalion, East Yorkshire Regiment, was captured by Germans in June 1942, shortly before Tobruk fell, and was handed over to the Italians. When the Italian surrender occurred on 8 September 1943, Billany and Dowie were freed from the camp in northern Italy to which they had been moved. It appears that they went first to Soragna, a small town near the prison camp; it was from there that the manuscripts of the novels were mailed by a farmer to Billany's father in 1946. One guesses that this was done when it became evident that the authors would not be returning to collect them. Billany and Dowie were seen in Mantova (Mantua) in December 1943. When *The Cage* was published in 1949 the dust-jacket carried a request for information about the authors. The publishers learned from a former fellow-prisoner that Billany was killed in 1945, near Fermo, by a British prisoner who had informed the Germans of the whereabouts of his own countrymen. 'Billany tried to put an end to the activities of this informer, and was mortally wounded in an encounter with him', reports a note to the Faber edition of *The Trap* (1986). The dust-jacket of the second impression of *The Cage* adds that Billany 'was accompanied in this attempt by another man of whom nothing has since been heard. Was this man Dowie?' That question remains unanswered. Fermo is on the Adriatic coast; it appears that the two men had been unable to reach Switzerland from Mantova and turned south in the hope of meeting the advancing British and American armies.

The Cage, the authors write, is intended to 'take you into the strange world where we have now been living for a year' (Billany and Dowie, 1949, p. 2); this would give June or July 1943 as the date of commencement, by which time they had been moved twice, from Capua north to Rezzanello near Piacenza in December 1942 ('as pleasant as any prison could be'), and on to Fontanellato near Parma at the end of March 1943. The manuscript, which is written in the hands of both men, was presumably begun at Fontanellato, and completed despite the overcrowded conditions and lack of privacy there.

The Cage is the outstanding instance of a fragmentary wartime text. The authors are fully aware that they are in the middle of things: 'for as we write this we are in it' (p. 2). The novel begins playfully, having nowhere to go. It opens by reproducing a letter from England that shows a comic inability to understand what imprisonment means ('See all those beautiful Cathedrals', p. 1). The contents of a Red Cross food parcel are listed, and the graffiti on the latrines described: 'No 4 latrine was the Chair in English Literature' (p. 21); confirmatory quotations are given. There are snatches of conversation, prison rumours, literary parodies and lines of verse, descriptions of the library (under someone's bed), of the Italian corporal, of the wall newspaper. It is an example of one of the oldest literary forms, the Roman *satura* or satire in which the author is free to bring in all kinds of writing – prose or verse – in pleasurable confusion. Such playfulness is not common in the English novel because it is inimical to moral seriousness.

The book was evidently begun without any sense of what its ending might be, and it is the authors' physical removal from one prison camp to another that eventually generates narrative momentum. Then comes the realization that experience determines style. After the first move, to Rezzanello, the authors realize that its new psychological conditions require a different kind of writing. Capua had been primarily the physical experience of adjustment to prison, whilst Rezzanello was to demand a psychological and emotional adjustment.

The new psychological circumstances mean that 'it is a quite different *type* of story we have to tell, and we have to use a different method to set it out' (p. 87); this brings in David's diary (which may be real or contrived), broken up by dramatized conversations concerning Alan's growing devotion to him. Finally, the Fontanellato experience is represented in a third way, sections headed 'David', 'Henry', 'Alan' or 'Dan' giving the interior monologues of each person as David and Alan's strained relationship reaches its resolution.

The novel describes the close emotional relationship between David and Alan. Homosexuality among male prisoners has been an impossible subject for war fiction, which is either resolutely heterosexual or silent on such matters. Eric Newby was also imprisoned at Fontanellato, at the same time as Billany and Dowie:

> Even more difficult for the residents in the *orfanotrofio* [orphanage] was any kind of homosexual act. Whatever loves there were between prisoners could only be expressed by looks and words or perhaps a surreptitious pressure of the hand, otherwise they had to remain locked away within the hearts and minds of the lovers. (Newby, 1975, pp. 46–7)

Newby then recommends *The Cage* on this subject.

David and Alan's physical intimacy amounts to no more than a single grasp of the hand; but it is not only for that reason that I feel that some caution is required before defining *The Cage* as a novel about homosexuality. Alan's difficulty is that in the prison camp, where there is no future, he cannot feel at all:

> The worst is at dead of night, when I wake suddenly in the dark and am aware of myself as an unused, unusable mechanism. I

touch my body and limbs and wonder why the heart should go on beating, the lungs breathing, when the whole machine runs for nothing . . . This body of mine is never used, never really lives . . . It's warm human life I lack. Generosity. Giving. Tenderness. (pp. 166, 167)

Alan is twenty-seven, a Communist, from David's and his own point of view excessively intellectual: 'My desert is arid with intellect' (p. 166). He wants and needs physical love: 'I want to be a man in my own right. And at the same time I want David's love' (p. 167). It is the resolution of this difficulty by a movement into feeling and away from intellect that emerges as the novel's subject.

The diary entries show Alan steadily pressing himself upon David, giving him cigarettes and long underwear. 'Though he can be very interesting intellectually', records David, 'I haven't any real affection for him' (p. 100). He asks outright why Alan is doing this:

ALAN: (*Long silence – walks with hands thrust into pockets and eyes on the path in front.*) Well; I suppose . . . if the words mean anything in such a case . . . I'm in love . . . in love with you.

DAVID: Um . . . (p. 102)

There the scene ends. David dislikes Alan because he clings to him: 'It's this utter servility, almost Uriah Heepish, which makes me distrust him and resent the whole relationship' (p. 107). Dan (a separate character and another side of Dan Billany, presumably), tells David that he has some responsibility for the situation: 'Ask yourself whether Alan's irritating humility isn't due to your lack of kindness. See a little bad in yourself, it may help you to see a little good in him' (p. 106). And David begins to change:

So I must carry him. I must let the light in. Open the gates and let Alan in. But I daren't because I don't trust him. Afraid of his needs. Afraid of the prospect of the unending sentimentality of an unsatisfied human being. Twenty-seven and never known the love of a woman . . . Oh, Alan, drop the mask, laugh; for God's sake, show guts; encourage me to help you. (p. 162)

After a drunken party (possible because the vermouth allowance could be saved), David begins to see Alan 'almost as a strong man overborne and broken' (p. 177), and holds his hand:

> I gripped his hand tightly and told him how sorry I was about it all. I told him, I remember, that he must see that I couldn't feel any different about him by sheer force of will; that it must come from him. (p. 178)

He is saying the right things. Alan realizes that he is looking for a mother-substitute, not a woman-substitute: 'I've been misunderstanding myself. Sex be damned' (p. 182). This realization changes his attitude towards David, who stops feeling oppressed: 'The Alan I hated was a falsehood' (p. 188), but the true Alan has genuine affection for him. Alan in his inexperience has called this affection 'love', so that David, who has loved women, had concluded that he had become an ' "unhealthy" ' ' "substitute for the women he's never had" '. (p. 189) As the extra quotation marks indicate, such feelings were clichéd and inexact. David had for months been treading down Alan's genuine regard, distorting it and preventing their relationship from succeeding. He regrets the lost months of friendship. Now there will be a change:

> The days that were coming would be better than those that had gone. I *would* take his hand. I *would* lead him back to the world of life. I never would desert him now till I had set him back on the road he had strayed from. We should not be fighting each other any more. For us the war was over. (p. 190)

The novel ends there, in this way resolving a complex dialectic of feeling in which each man changes because the other has shown himself capable of change. The final sentence alludes to the phrase sometimes used when fighting men were captured; it occurs in *The Trap*: 'You Kaput, for you the war is over' (p. 345). Its use here does not imply the capture of one man by the other, but marks the end of an unnecessary struggle and the establishment of a new mutuality of affection between Alan and David.

Because there is only one sex in the prison, it is difficult to say that either man has *chosen* homosexuality, for if they are to love at all, it must be with a person of the same sex. This is a heterosexual's solution to the problem of love in a single-sex society. Known as 'deprivation homosexuality' it was 'not an uncommon practice among men of otherwise heterosexual disposition' (Costello, 1985, p. 159). Nevertheless, because there is to be touching and holding – as the physical signs of affection and shared regard – we must recognize that there is here an admirable extension of the often limited male capacity for feeling.

These changes in feeling take place in a political context. The fall of Mussolini, the slow approach of the British and American forces, even the Fascist architecture of the orphanage itself, are all kept in view, so that life is shown as being lived within politics. The authors go further:

> Philosophers interpret the world, but it is also necessary to change it. To recognize that one is childish is only the beginning of the job; it is also necessary to grow up. (p. 181)

These are Alan's thoughts. The allusion in the first sentence is to the eleventh of Marx's Theses on Feuerbach: 'The philosophers have only *interpreted* the world, in various ways; the point is to *change* it.' To introduce this quotation at the point where Alan is becoming capable of change suggests that the authors were trying to relate their own concern with subjectivity to Marx's similar concern: the Theses argue the primacy of 'sensuous human activity' and the social construction of the subject.

The allusion makes it possible to read the relationship between Alan and David as political rather than 'moral' (as that term might be understood in the criticism of novels by George Eliot, for example). The dialectic of change which both men undergo as they resolve their feelings for each other can be understood as an attempt to apply Marx's materialist philosophy of the dialectic to personal relations. It is difficult to judge whether the novel succeeds in doing this; but it can be said that it integrates the relationship of love with its political and sexual-political context. The Alan–David relationship has meaning because it occurs within, but is different from, the political and sexual relationships surrounding it.

The Cage, then, is a playful and structurally disintegrated text in which all the varied elements function to define the transformations undergone by Alan's and David's subjectivity. The conditions of war and the loss of freedom have created material circumstances in which the subject can be changed, and will go on changing. 'The days that were coming would be better than those that had gone.' (p. 190) That hope for the future of unfree subjects may also be a hope for the futures of many differently related subjects, also transformed by the conditions of war. The implicit proposition is that subjective change initiates political change.

Dan Billany's war novels both have titles that suggest the imposition of some kind of control. In *The Cage* the constraint is obvious and immediate, but in *The Trap* the sense of being caught is more various and is dispersed across several decades of pre-war English history. The novel begins just before the First World War, traverses the intervening years of slump and unemployment, and ends in the fighting in North Africa in 1942, where Michael Carr, the novel's speaking 'I', is captured and imprisoned. But this is not a conventional first-person narrative, despite the opening line: 'There I stood, looking at the letter' (Billany, 1986, p. 11). Where he stood is not identified, and will not be until the novel's final page. The opening continues by telling, not the life story of 'I', but the lives of his girlfriend Elizabeth's parents (John and Marion Pascoe), and then the life of Elizabeth herself and her marriage to Michael. The first person singular is always somewhere present in this telling, commenting and ordering the narration; but in doing this 'I' undermines the conventional first-person narration by recording events at which he was not or could not have been present (many occur before his birth). The descriptions of Elizabeth's own early life are recorded with a detail that she could not herself have provided in telling them. This produces an unusual effect: the narrator's concern with the details of a life he could not have known confirms for the reader his love for Elizabeth. Feeling is implied by the conduct of the narrative.

The slowly growing prosperity of Elizabeth's parents is measured by the accumulation of small domestic necessities, and the home life they build together. The house to which Michael Carr comes is at Polpryn (Penryn) near Helston in Cornwall. There are tensions within the family, 'but all identified themselves very closely with the house and with each other' (p. 77). That house is destroyed by a sea mine dropped during a raid in 1941, and the family's intimate life is destroyed with it. Elizabeth and Michael hurriedly marry and rent a house for the family; but it is 'just a temporary shelter, not a home. There were no household gods in it at all' (p. 183). Michael is immediately sent abroad, travels by sea to Egypt, takes part in the fighting in Libya, and is captured. The novel ends with the arrival at the Italian prison camp of a letter from Elizabeth. This is the letter mentioned on the novel's first page. *The Trap* is written out of a deep desire for change, but also with a bitter recognition that people's hopes are always unfulfilled; like the Pascoes, most people go through life wondering why it has failed them.

The Trap is suffused with the sense of impermanence. Billany is acutely conscious that economic and political activity is a contrivance, a made thing that is a human structure, its solidity an illusion. 'To see the same trading company or travel agency which one knew in a grey street in the North of England, open its chrome-plate doors and windows under the hot blue dome of Africa, is to be teased out of thought by the singular invisible root from which both grew.' It shows 'the pleasant hollowness of our solidity' (p. 217). The transitory life of men travelling to war instances this hollowness: the base camps in the empty desert, the positions taken up and abandoned during fighting.

The moment that demonstrates this hollowness most fearfully occurs when Carr and his men have been captured and they watch from the German lines a counter-attack being made *towards* them by Captain Burgess and H.Q. Company. The effect is sufficiently disorientating to be worth quoting at length:

I could see each individual section of the attacking platoons . . . Burgess, pistol in hand, was running in front of them. Running with one leg stiff; he must have been wounded already. Serious faces. They could see Death running to meet them . . . Burgess half-turned – only seventy yards from me – shouted 'Charge'.

Down came the bayonets to the 'on guard', I even heard the involuntary cry of the men as they sprang forward to the last assault. Simultaneously the German guns roared, in less than ten seconds I saw half the company fall. Death struck them on the run, they bowled headlong like schoolboys stumbling in a race, they fell with the crash of their helmets, equipment and rifles . . . Burgess still ran. He was only twenty yards away now. He could feel his men still at his back. But now the situation changed very quickly. Because of the unremitting German fire, there simply were not enough men left to charge . . . While some of the Germans continued to fire, others jumped up on their feet and shouted to our men to surrender, calling 'Kamarad'. Burgess stopped, glanced back at the few men with him, turned to the enemy again, and aimed his pistol at a German soldier standing near me. The German brought his rifle to the shoulder: Burgess fired twice, the German once. Burgess fell flat on his back. Later I saw that the bullet had entered his face between the nose and the upper lip. (pp. 348–9)

Battle is usually seen from the point of view of either attacker or attacked, with the observer's emotions engaged upon one side or the other. Here the observer is dispassionate. Burgess has chosen not to live, and has made the same decision for his men. The incident is disturbing because the unusual point of view allows Carr to admire the courage and organization of Burgess and H.Q. Company, and also observe the skilful rifleman and the Germans who invite surrender. The assumption that in battle we are exclusively engaged on one side or the other is here undermined. The very business of fighting is revealed as another contrived human activity. It belongs with all those other structures through which we attempt to order our lives and control others.

The Trap is not as conspicuously broken up as is The Cage, but similar principles are at work. There are frequent authorial interventions. These may take the form of an aphoristic sentence, a paragraph, or an entire chapter. The narrative does not move forward freely, except during the fighting scenes towards the end. If The Cage begins playfully and becomes more serious, The Trap is throughout reflective and reflexive, commenting on the world it creates and upon its own procedures.

On the very first page of the novel the authorial 'I' raises the question of what distance should be established between the authorial persona and the reader. Hemingway excludes the reader too severely, but R. L. Stevenson is too amiable, whilst William Saroyan affects a Chaplinesque naïvety (pp. 11–12). Of these, Hemingway presents the greatest threat to Billany's project: 'I'm scared to fall into that style, because it's so near to what I want to do' (p. 11). He wishes to write about events – often violent, as in Hemingway – at the same time as commenting upon them in a way that will involve the reader. The authorial 'I' (which I take to be close to Billany, perhaps identical with him) holds a point of view, itself changing, which is intended to change the attitude of the reader. Hemingway also implies an attitude towards his subject, but it is not one that invites the reader's involvement. The characters in Hemingway to whom we are expected to attend are already formed before the beginning of the novels in which they appear. They are automata set loose in the fiction, working out their natures but learning nothing. What they know, they already know; what they do derives from this knowledge, but all we are shown is their actions. They make blunders and errors in their struggle with the physical world, and it is the consequences of these often stupid actions which give the novels their interest. Hemingway's minimalist style gives a definiteness to speech and action that continually informs the reader that there could have been no alternative words or deeds. There is no space for reflection in the minds of Hemingway's characters, and no space between text and reader allowing the latter to operate with critical freedom upon the text. Consequently there could hardly be a worse model than Hemingway for a writer wishing to make his novel a critique of action, rather than simply a description of action itself.

Writing in Hemingway's shadow, Billany's difficulty was to create a reflective 'I', capable of change, who is at the same time sufficiently decisive to command other men in battle. When the platoon's final positions are about to be overrun by tanks, Carr survives mentally because he cannot believe that what is happening is real. The only fixed realities are those of childhood; every subsequent experience has been part of a process of change:

> All those [childhood] things happened to a real me in a real world which I didn't make and was none of my choosing. But since then I had led life after life, each one more chosen and more consciously willed by myself, and each one *less real* . . . the earlier realities were deeper in me, fixed, immovable, not to be changed in the least by all the different elements I later chose to swim in. (p. 336)

Shortly afterwards an armoured car comes into range, its observer visible in the turret. ' "Shoot him in the belly" ', orders Carr (p. 341). The sensitivity of the reflective passage is not inconsistent with Carr's ability to command; both activities are chosen, both can be done with conviction.

The successful combination of contemplation and action in *The Trap* is the outcome of a prose method that is self-aware but not self-conscious, and owes nothing to the techniques of modernism. Billany successfully fulfils the project he sets himself at the outset: 'a sober, strong attitude to my writing, yet a sensitiveness' (p. 11). This is an instance of English plain style, the mode of direct, uncomplicated address that runs from Defoe, through Fielding and 'Mark Rutherford' down to Orwell's essays and Edward Upward's fiction. It is a style that has always been able to carry radical meanings, for as it speaks to people, it speaks for them as well.

Carr spends a great deal of time trying to humanize one of his men, Frank Shaw, an eighteen-year-old with the mind of a boy of fourteen. Shaw is incompetent, insubordinate, gets drunk and violent, is court-martialled for going AWOL, and imprisoned. His truculence conceals his vulnerability. Carr addresses him as 'Frank' and tries to gain his confidence. In the desert he tells Shaw what the stars are, what the sun is, and about the relationship between the earth and the moon. 'Shaw was rapt. "Nobody's ever told me such things. I could listen to things like that for ever" ' (p. 260). Billany's control of the plain style prevents this scene, and others showing his good relations with his men, from becoming sentimental. During the fighting Shaw finds his role alongside the other men, and as capture becomes imminent suggests Carr should remove his pips and go into captivity with them. When Shaw is shot after capture, a relationship is broken:

> I was dumb and bewildered: here was his flesh, solid and real to my touch, and his clothes, yet I could not say anything more to him, ever: could not tell him I was sorry I had not saved him after all. The same hands, the same limbs, yet he wasn't there. Touching meant nothing. (p. 350)

To the army, Shaw is rubbish; to his officer he matters intensely, partly for reasons of military efficiency, but predominantly because he is another human being who can be valued across the division between 'officer' and 'other ranks', so much so that he can be touched.

Billany does not interpret the war as a People's War that would eventually transform the struggling lives of such people as the Pascoes. For him the war continues by other means the economic and political policies of the 1920s and 1930s, the very policies which had initially defeated them, and multitudes like them. The course of the war itself does not offer hope for the future, but the people who fight it do, whether it is the Shaws in the desert or the Pascoes at home. The war is conducted in hope, but hope is always deferred. During the desert fighting Carr dreams that he is a boy again, about to drink from a bottle that would give him 'the secret of life, the potency and fulfilment we live for and die without' (p. 310); but the liquid will not flow and he is awoken for a battle conference. He feels cheated of 'a colossal fulfilment, or an orgasm' (p. 311). It is this larger pessimism about all purposive activities, together with a matching optimism about individuals, that accounts for the ending of the novel.

The final chapter consists of a translation of the instructions to the guards at the Capua prison camp, rather in the manner of *The Cage*, and a reflective passage expressing weariness with war emotions: 'The war emotions are frivolous . . . The war is as ridiculous as Sweeney Todd, the Demon Barber. It is not related to the true feelings of real people. Only the sufferings are real. The causes for which we suffer are contemptible and ridiculous.' Billany never describes the war as anti-Fascist. He comes close to saying that the war is not worth fighting because both sides are capitalist and the conflict merely prolongs the sufferings of such people as the Pascoes. The resolution comes with the arrival of Carr's first letter from his wife Elizabeth, the letter he has been expecting throughout the campaign, 'the letter which meant for me the worst of it was over'. Personal relations between loving individuals are more important than the emotions of war: 'I do not "believe" in the war – in this or any other' (p. 380).

It is possible that Billany interpreted the war as an imperialist war between capitalist states in which it was not possible to take sides. This was a position adopted in 1939 by the European Communist parties, and abandoned only when the Nazi–Soviet pact was broken by the invasion of the Soviet Union in 1941. Although the 'imperialist war' line ceased to be official policy, there is no reason why individuals should not have continued to hold it, despite the ridicule it attracted, even from the Left. Perhaps it was a view that could only legitimately be held by someone who had fought the war with the conviction shown by Michael Carr.

One of the tones of Billany's discourse is anger. In a remarkable passage this anger is directed against 'the sweating, multifarious work' then going on throughout the world to kill, imprison and destroy. It is the swearing of a modern oath:

By the blood of those I loved who have died, by the years of my own life which have been taken from me, I swear I shall never again from humility acquiesce in the martyrdom of man, never again believe in the cunning sophistication of the world, its vulgar ignorant self-certainty, its cant and its sly admissions. I have seen the wise old world at its work: Folly and Falseness like two foul doctors poisoning their patient. The Worldly Wisdom which engendered the war was just this: Self-Interest, deliberate blindness, gay ignorance that climbs to fortune treading on its neighbour's face: and all the quackery and political-economic mumbo-jumbo which is necessary to mask and justify these things. From now on till I die I shall not cease to smash my fist into the vacant, grinning face of our cant civilization, never cease from crying 'UNCLEAN!', never cease from pointing to the blood and bones of murdered men. (pp. 365-6)

This oath is probably the finest expression of anger against the war to occur in recent English war fiction. It is a personal statement whose formality and allusiveness give it the power of an immense generalization. The capitalized vices derive from Bunyan's *Pilgrim's Progress*, the repeated 'I shall not cease' from Blake's 'Jerusalem' ('I shall not cease from mental fight'), the image of smashing a fist in civilization's face from inter-war Communist rhetoric, the cry of 'unclean' from the Bible, where it is made by lepers. These allusions give to this curse such substance that it becomes the expresssion of a vast collective anger.

English fiction can always admit characters who are angry for specific reasons, and readers may become angry reading of injustices suffered by the innocent. Angry authors are a different matter, for they demand an assent that we may not be prepared to give. In *The Trap* anger is provoked when the achievements of hard work are destroyed, and immense labour goes into the cruelly misapplied work of destruction. Billany links the suspect emotion, anger, to the excluded subject, work. In terms of the English novel this is a double transgression, but in terms of the war novel it is entirely fitting. War is work, anger the emotion with which we should confront war.

The Trap brings together more successfully than any wartime fiction the themes that I am exploring in this book. The war is interpreted not as an isolated episode but in an historical perspective, whilst its causes are subjected to a socialist critique by a working-class author (and narrator) who is prepared to express his anger at what he finds. 'The Present is a room; the Past furnishes it, the Future lights it' (p. 50). This aphorism describes the conceptual structure of *The Trap* itself, and it is against the implications of this structure that other war novels should be

judged. If these novels offer no past, then the present they describe
must be deficient; if they offer no future (the strategy of Anthony
Powell) then they cannot tell the truth about the present.

The invasion of Normandy in June 1944 is the climactic moment
in the People's War. The beginning of the final attack on Germany, it was also the beginning of the end of the war. After this,
the looked-for future became possible. The invasion was also
intended to relieve the pressure upon the Soviet forces which were
approaching Germany from the east; since 1941 Stalin had been
asking for a Second Front to be opened, and the refusal to provide
it had become a cause of stress in relations with the Soviet Union.
Stalin could plausibly argue that it was his armies that were doing
the hard work. The Second Front was therefore a political issue to
which the Left in Britain was particularly committed. Naomi
Mitchison records in her diary a friend's remark: 'Would people
afterwards ever know what "Second Front" meant to us emotionally, how much we wanted it [?]' (Mitchison, p. 283). During the
post-war years this feeling has been quietly forgotten. Cornelius
Ryan, in his well-known account of D-Day, *The Longest Day*
(1960), omits to mention the political reasons. By contrast, the
authors of the two novels of Normandy that I shall now turn to
are both sharply aware of the full reasons for the invasion.

Alexander Baron's *From the City, From the Plough* is a novel of
the People's Army. It shows a multitude of characters, men of the
5th Battalion of the imaginary Wessex Regiment, as they prepare
for D-Day and as they fight their way through the beautiful
bocage country towards Caen. It is a novel of collective experience intended as a response to post-war 'officer novels'. David
Holbrook's *Flesh Wounds* (1966) is a novel of individual experience. It traces a longer period, from Paul Grimmer's initial
training as an officer, through Normandy, and into his post-war
return to Cambridge University as an undergraduate. A socialist,
Paul Grimmer knows that he will be taking part in the Second
Front. An exchange with a girlfriend indicates the political consequences of the entry of Russia into the war:

'A year ago you'd have gone to jail as a pacifist. Now the Left has all swung around.'

'Well, there you are – since Russia. We've done it now.'

The Left is committed to the war about which it had been doubtful; and again the Spanish Civil War imposes itself as the Left's model of action, for the image to follow is of John Cornford, the Cambridge political activist and writer who had died in Spain: ' "You all want to go like that," ' Paul's girlfriend remarks (Holbrook, 1966, p. 8).

These are both novels of action, and both show how male sexuality is implicated in action. Baron has too many characters to allow any of them to develop very greatly, but some find roles for themselves in battle that they cannot find in civilian life. Holbrook, with a single central character – whose experience is close to his own – is free to trace the changes in Paul Grimmer's identity that occur in training and in fighting.

Baron shows the strength of feeling that can exist between men. We may feel some sentimentality in the description of Number Nine Platoon going to bed: 'There was warmth and trust and tenderness and loving-kindness in this hut' (Baron, 1979, p. 29), but it is an extension of male feeling akin to that found in Billany's and Dowie's *The Cage*. The same feeling occurs when Major Maddison finds a corpse in his riflemen's trench. It 'belongs' to another battalion:

'Get the bloody thing out of here,' said Maddison curtly, 'before it stinks.'

'Yes, sir,' said the corporal, not moving . . .

'Don't forget,' he said again, 'get the stiff out of the way before it's daylight.' He walked away.

'Whoreson,' said the corporal. He knelt by the corpse and gently replaced the blanket over the waxen face.

'Some poor mother'll be weeping for this lad,' he said tenderly. (pp. 147–8)

Such feelings as these are shared by Colonel Pothecary, an able commander whose weakness, in the view of his superiors, is that he likes his men. He suffers when they are killed, and cannot treat them only as a matter for report forms and burial arrangements. His own son missing at sea, he sympathizes with the families of his men as they await bad news. This feeling for others, amongst the men and from a no doubt untypical officer, indicates the novel's argument that the war is worth winning only in terms of human sympathy and mutual care.

The argument is developed through the same Major Maddison who has such contempt for the bodies of dead soldiers. Maddison is 'the Mad Major', much hated by the men, whom he drives hard. He too has a love for the men, but it is the love of a repressed homosexual:

> When a platoon came streaming over a wall like a pack of hounds, Major Maddison would feel excited and close to them; [when he sees them in the showers] he would grow exultant with emotions which he could not fathom and would walk away flushed with love for these men of his – until . . . he would see a soldier strolling with his girl and would feel sick and contemptuous once more. (pp. 66–7)

One night he wakes up the half-asleep guardroom by throwing in a training grenade. When Colonel Pothecary criticizes this behaviour Maddison defends himself by pointing out that these men would be fighting a highly trained German army: ' "Soldiers, Spartans, trained and hardened from boyhood, as men should be trained, ruthless and fearless and in love with death" ' (p. 65). As for the British, there is 'not a warrior among them', to which remark Pothecary replies: ' "Thank God for that . . . Warriors indeed!" ' (p. 66). In Normandy it turns out that the German soldiers are indeed better trained than the British, and to that extent Maddison is justified. But his lunatic behaviour, putting himself and his men at risk during reconnaissance, leads to his own death. He is shot by his own sergeant after his Bren carrier is overturned by a near-hit from an 88mm shell (p. 166). Such men as Maddison, with attitudes indistinguishable from those of the enemy, have no place in a future that should be defined by love and tenderness. It is towards such a future that the men of the Wessex Regiment are fighting in Normandy.

Flesh Wounds is also future-directed, and uses the erotic as one means of discovering why the future is valuable. But before that point is reached the innocent and inexperienced undergraduate Paul Grimmer has to become a soldier. His training at Battle School under the ferocious but effective Sergeant MacAllcane comes as a shock, but his new identity as a soldier is established, to the extent that his girlfriend Lucy does not at first recognize him. 'A crude animal energy took the place of his more tender feelings, and he came to despise the soft life of those outside the barrack walls, those . . . who did not carry a pistol at the belt' (p. 64). He has been hardened enough for the relationship with Lucy to end, but his new self is not sufficiently secure to endure being under fire for the first time. Caught outside his tank by a mortar attack, his feelings are of personal disintegration:

> He swore never to be caught out of a closed tank again: he lost every conviction, political, moral, human: he would have capitulated to any enemy, believed in any God he had been required to believe in – if only the reward were to be relieved from the terror of the falling spate of mortar bombs. (p. 136).

He divides himself from himself, body from mind: 'His intellect exercised fantastic feats of detachment, seeking to survive' (p. 136). The identity created for him by the army begins to break:

> 'The mortaring had already crazed the thin fabric of his youthful determined allegiance to the Army' (p. 141). Most significantly of all, Paul loses something from his own essential identity. Lying on the ground, he has watched a beetle crawl towards a clod of earth (if the beetle gets there, he will survive – it does). He tells his driver to avoid stepping on it. ' "Are you all right, Sir?" ' the driver asks, and they laugh; but Paul wonders if he is mad, and how long anyone could be sane under such circumstances. Some 'wholeness in his identity' has been lost: 'It was now as if one self would always be poised, ready to desert the other, in extreme situations. He felt inwardly split, demoralized, disloyal' (p. 138).

It is very unusual for writers of Second World War fiction to recognize that permanent damage to the personality can be caused by being under fire or in other difficult situations caused by war. Writers of popular fiction do not allow the possibility at all: tiredness, exhaustion and even stress can be acknowledged, but not any fundamental mental disturbance. Nor do more serious writers often admit to this feeling, though there is an instance in Eric Newby's account of his life among Italian peasants after the surrender in 1943. He is in a group crossing a mountainside:

> That night something happened to me on the mountain. The weight of the rice coupled with the awful cough which I had to try and repress broke something in me. It was not physical; it was simply that part of my spirit went out of me, and in the whole of my life since that night it has never been the same again. (Newby, 1975, p. 286)

The war caused immense mental and spiritual distress, but apart from a melodramatic instance in Nigel Balchin's *Mine Own Executioner* (1945) very little has been written about this. Spike Milligan's moving description of the beginnings of his own manic-depressive illness in *Mussolini: His Part in My Downfall* is an exception. The immediate cause is an attack by mortars (which seem to have had a particular ability to cause alarm, perhaps because their trajectory means they are not heard until the last moment). Milligan, suffering from piles and after three nights without sleep and seventeen hours operating a radio from an Observation Post, is asked to carry batteries and a radio set to another OP. He retreats under mortar fire and, slightly wounded, is taken off in an ambulance, in tears. He is returned to his unit a week later, reduced from lance-bombardier to gunner by the same major who had originally ordered the OP expedition, and put back to work. A day later he leaves for hospital: 'As I drove back down that muddy mountain road, with the morning mists filling the valleys, I felt as though I was being taken across the Styx. I've never got over that feeling' (Milligan, 1980, p. 285). Again the experience causes a permanent loss of spirit, as in Newby and Holbrook.

Holbrook's novel shows a recognition that battle-weariness is directly related to sexual desire. Paul Grimmer crosses to the Rhineland, and is given leave in Brussels where he spends several unhappy days struggling with 'the hallucinations of desire' (p. 223). Eventually he meets a woman who spontaneously takes him in, feeds him and loves him. Their lovemaking restores his faith in the future:

> In his mind, he felt blissfully relaxed by the clasp of another body all that night, and felt solutions coming to the questions which that winter had dogged his hopes for the end of the war – 'What for?' 'What does one survive *for*?' She brought the answer home to him – the strange generous girl on whose pillow he lay. That one night's warmth more than compensated for all that he had suffered . . . The Belgian girl's *amitié* restored his faith in human nature, and his hope, by the renewed experience of what joy could be. (p. 229)

Here the sense of the future is expressed in personal terms which we are to understand will also extend to the political, in a refreshed sense of the possibilities for human nature.

This I take to be the true conclusion of Holbrook's novel, which – in a further twenty pages – returns to Cambridge and Paul's attempt to find a relationship there. We are told that he rejects a girl because he wants a 'whole relationship' rather than the 'brief satisfaction of the soldier's hunger' (p. 251); no doubt this is preferable, but the relationship in Brussels, in which the young man with the damaged identity is restored by just such a 'brief satisfaction', is far more persuasive.

IV

The Post-war Epic

The large-scale works of fiction published after the war was over – in most cases, many years after – make special claims as interpretations of the entire conflict. By writing of the war in trilogies or as part of longer novel sequences, Anthony Powell, Evelyn Waugh, C. P. Snow and Olivia Manning invoke the authority that accrues to inclusiveness, to the leisurely and detailed overview whose impressive formal structure indicates that a significant act of interpretation is in progress. These fictions imply a different kind of understanding from the tentative claims made by the fragmentary and time-bound works written during the war. The post-war 'epics' offer themselves as a form of knowledge about the war, a version of history. Two of these epics, those by Snow and Manning, have been adapted for television, so that a further cultural authority is attached to them. Few of the novels I have discussed so far have a presence in the culture comparable to these. This fiction covers a very wide range of diverse experience, but it has one broad tendency: to suppress or to limit all those hopeful political expectations and personal freedoms that the war years made possible. My subject in this chapter is the strategies – narrative, political and personal – by which this is achieved.

Every one of these novel sequences is autobiographical, and each has as narrator or dominant point of view a figure whose experiences are known to follow closely those of the author. Yet in reworking their own lives these authors do not attempt to reproduce themselves as dominant personalities. Three sequences, those by Powell, Waugh and Snow, have narrators who share one remarkable quality, their weak presence. It is difficult to find anywhere else in English literature a more retiring, diffident and self-negating gathering than Powell's Nicholas Jenkins, Waugh's Guy Crouchback and Snow's Lewis Eliot. Although the dominant point of view in Olivia Manning's two trilogies is Harriet Pringle, the centre of interest is her husband Guy. This semi-invisible male set at one remove from the reader is brother to Jenkins, Crouchback and Eliot.

Why should there be so many indistinct men in these novels? Nicholas Jenkins is ineffectual, Guy Crouchback is a suffering emptiness, Lewis Eliot a force without content, Guy Pringle a hyperactive enigma. This lack of definition is an aspect of the paradox that makes possible these novels' claim to be authoritative. Because well-defined figures must behave 'in character', their range of possible responses is limited. Weakly defined narrators can undergo all kinds of experience, absorb it and respond to it and still seem plausible because the reader has a restricted sense of how they 'ought' to behave. Such empty figures are particularly valuable vehicles for an author who requires that one character should undergo very varied experiences, of the kind met with in wartime. The war caused great mental and physical stress, raised new and difficult moral questions and created unprecedented political conjunctions. In these conditions an 'empty' character allows continuity of consciousness where there is a marked discontinuity in action. Such continuity, attached to the range of experience, amounts to a claim of special authority.

If the men are indistinct, the women in these sequences are vivid. Yet they are all judged. Powell's Pamela Flitton is promiscuous, Waugh's Virginia Troy is married four times (twice to Guy), Snow's Sheila Knight is mentally unbalanced and Manning's Harriet Pringle appears to have no sexual relations with her husband. All are extreme cases of one kind and another. Waugh suggests that Virginia is a figure from romance:

> 'Virginia was the last of them – the exquisite, the doomed, and the damning, with expiring voices . . . We shall never see anyone like her again in literature or in life and I'm very glad to have known her.' (Waugh, 1984, p. 541)

Virginia is a *femme fatale*, and so is Pamela Flitton. These women can disturb men, and are therefore praised for their vivacity but isolated for their promiscuity. Pamela is subjected to a barrage of attack, overwhelmingly sexual in content:

> 'I only stuffed her once,' said Duport. 'Against a shed in the back parts of Cairo airport, but even then I could see she might drive you round the bend, if she really decided to.' (Powell, 1971, p. 195)

Later Pamela uses the phrase, ' "Stuff the Ambassador" ' and Nicholas thinks, 'The phrase recalled Duport' (p. 214). In this way Duport's attitude to Pamela, rather than being criticized, is integrated into the novel's complex system of cross-references.

There is one exhilarating moment in Waugh's *Men at Arms* when Virginia vehemently asserts herself against Guy. Guy, a Roman Catholic, has recently discovered that even though he is divorced from her it would not be a sin to resume sexual relations. She becomes furiously angry:

> 'I thought you'd taken a fancy to me again and wanted a bit of fun for the sake of old times. I thought you'd chosen me specially, and by God you had. Because I was the only woman in the whole world your priests would let you go to bed with. That was my attraction. You wet, smug, obscene, pompous, sexless, lunatic pig.' (p. 104)

There is a plain contrast between male characters who are indistinct but in touch with important matters, and women who are clearly defined but difficult.

The war caused marked changes in sexual behaviour and in the balance of relations between men and women. In these novels we can see a post-war effort to reinterpret those changes and wherever possible to negate them when they favour women. Whatever spectacular sexual events occur, all reach conventional conclusions about moral and sexual behaviour. Harriet, for example, reaches the submissive conclusion that 'In an imperfect world, marriage was a matter of making do with what one had chosen' (Manning, 1982, p. 566).

The act of reinterpretation extends beyond the sexual. Each sequence opposes, implicitly or explicitly, the attitudes and arguments supporting the People's War version of events. Anthony Powell writes with detached wit about army life, but cannot allow his characters any consideration of the future. Evelyn Waugh's trilogy is an amusing and skilfully constructed record of wartime attitudes and behaviour; but his overall purpose is to break down the concept of a People's War, particularly as it drew strength from changed working-class attitudes and from the alliance with the Soviet Union. C. P. Snow dramatizes the attitudes to politics and moral questions among a group of influential scientists but through Lewis Eliot he is also concerned to legitimize the work of the Civil Service and assert the values of a functioning bureaucracy, and Olivia Manning subjects the future-directed People's War politics of Guy Pringle to a sustained criticism.

Before considering these novel sequences, I want to discuss *The Cruel Sea*, which was published in 1951, before any of the 'sequence' novels. This is a post-war epic in which action predominates as it does not in the later novels, but which nevertheless deals with the People's War theme and with the question of how women should be represented in war fiction. Nicholas Monsarrat's novel shows how post-war attitudes were beginning to change from those developed during the war itself. His politics (like Snow's) were liberal, whereas Powell's, Waugh's and Manning's were conservative. Post-war disillusion and the Cold War gave the latter the opportunity to reinterpret the war in terms relevant to the political needs of their own times, but Monsarrat's novel is an example of the immediate post-war pressure against change being reflected back over the war years.

The Cruel Sea tells the story of Lieutenant-Commander Ericson, experienced, tough, a natural leader of men, and Second-Lieutenant Lockhart, inexperienced but able to learn, as they command the corvette *Compass Rose* during Atlantic convoys. *Compass Rose* is sunk in 1942, during the worst period of the Battle of the Atlantic, and the two men, now promoted, take the frigate *Saltash* on further convoys. The major theme is dedication to the business of being effective in war: ' "you have to be single-minded, free of distraction, tough, untender – all the words that don't go with marriage. Otherwise you'll fail" ', Lockhart tells his girlfriend (Monsarrat, 1951, pp. 314–5). When men are distracted by difficulties in their home lives, their performance as fighting men is adversely affected: by means of this argument private life and the responsibilities of fighting are brought together.

Monsarrat had nearly become a Communist during the 1930s, had broadly radical sympathies during the war, was a Labour councillor immediately after it, and regarded himself as a liberal in South Africa, where he wrote *The Cruel Sea* during 1948–50. The novel is not illiberal, but numerous details show how it was possible to forget wartime ways of thinking and with only a slightly altered emphasis transform them into something less generous and less understanding.

The Cruel Sea is partly based on experiences described in *Three Corvettes*, short fragmentary works based on diaries that Monsarrat had published during the war. In *Three Corvettes* Monsarrat describes how he made the Beveridge Report available on board ship, and was upset that there was so little interest in it. In *The Cruel Sea* a lecture on war aims and the post-war world arouses no interest whatever among the crew of *Saltash*, and junior officers show indifference to the question of why they are fighting; but these attitudes now appear to have authorial approval (pp. 399–402). Lockhart – a version of the author – has gained 'in self-discipline, in responsibility, in simple confidence and the rout of fear' (p. 403); personal male virtue is the objective, no longer accompanied by public responsibilities.

The work theme, present in so many war novels, recurs here, Monsarrat remaining impressed by the way amateurs become sailors, transformed by their work; but this admiration is now attached to a superior 'Englishness':

> You could pour Englishmen – any Englishmen – into a ship, and they made that ship work and fight as if they had been doing it all their lives, catching up, overtaking, and leaving behind the professionals of any other nation. It was the basic virtue of living on an island. (p. 259)

This sympathy for the men is set off against a thoroughgoing contempt for women. In *Three Corvettes* Monsarrat had complained that problems on shore harmed fighting effectiveness. In *The Cruel Sea* this theme becomes obsessive. Sailors are undermined by bad marriages and bad sex; unfaithful women harm the war effort itself. Apart from Ericson's wife and Lockhart's girlfriend, every woman described in the novel is unfaithful or harmful. A promiscuous actress laughs at the news of her husband's death, a seaman goes absent hunting for his wife, a young officer catches venereal disease. The men in this novel fight two battles: one at sea against U-boats, another at home against women. *The Cruel Sea* is pervasively sexist.

Sex also determines which characters live and which must die. When *Compass Rose* is sunk, some die well, moral and hardworking to the last, but others die for sexual reasons. Sub-Lieutenant Baker has untreated venereal disease, and welcomes death in the agreeably numbing water. Stoker Evans is a bigamist, and chooses to die because he cannot face the complications. Lieutenant Morell thinks all night about his unfaithful wife, decides he has been a fool, and gives up. This is a stark example of the way in which authors of popular war fiction find 'moral' reasons for deciding which characters are to die and which to survive, in situations where death or survival is a matter of chance. There is the additional advantage that women can be blamed for the deaths of men in mid-Atlantic.

In its formal structure *The Cruel Sea* shows how difficult it is to attempt to cover the entire war in one volume. It is plausible that *Compass Rose* should be sunk in 1942, when German success in the Atlantic was at its height, but the novel is by then nearly three-quarters over. The awkward year of 1943, in which so little happened to which fiction can attach itself, is largely covered by the commissioning of the new ship, and the beginning of Lockhart's affair. The real excitement ended in 1942. Coverage of 1944 is perfunctory, and in May 1945 the rock-like hero Ericson can at last admit, ' "I must say I'm damned tired" ' (p. 416). Fragmentary episodes occur, but are sharply diminished in comparision with *Three Corvettes*. The novel is an attempt to structure the war, and to interpret it in the epic terms of heroism, action and personal achievement.

The Cruel Sea represents a tradition of popular writing to which the 'literary' novel sequences – to which I now return – do not belong. Anthony Powell's wartime novels have no heroes and show us no action. This is prepared for in a conversation between Nicholas Jenkins and Pennistone in the first volume of the trilogy. They are discussing the memoirs of the French poet Alfred de Vigny, who was in the army for fourteen years but never saw action. This, suggests Pennistone, may be the best way to investigate army life: '"Action is, after all, exciting rather than interesting"' (Powell, 1973, p. 114). In Powell's war novels the only triumphs are social and bureaucratic.

The war years are the subject of volumes 7, 8 and 9 of the twelve-volume sequence *A Dance to the Music of Time* (1951–75). The first of this inner sequence is *The Valley of Bones* (1964), which takes Nicholas Jenkins from the beginning of the war to just before the fall of Paris (13 June 1940). *The Soldier's Art* (1966) begins in December 1940 and ends with the German invasion of the Soviet Union on 22 June 1941. This is very leisurely. *The Military Philosophers* (1968) runs from 1941 to demobilization in 1945, the wide time-span made possible by a jump from May 1943 to July 1944. Most of the troublesome year, 1943, together with its awkward appendage, pre-Normandy 1944, is left out. James Tucker points out in *The Novels of Anthony Powell* (1976) that Powell's novels are notable for their almost complete lack of forward narrative movement. The political consequences of this narrative procedure require examination.

The near-stasis of Powell's fiction is partly the result of its complexity. There are three main layers in the war novels. First, the many characters who have appeared in earlier volumes of the sequence. Prominent among them are Kenneth Widmerpool, the elusive villain who works hard for power, and uses it to dispose – and dispose of – the lives of long-standing friends of Nicholas's, notably Charles Stringham and Peter Templer. (By administrative means Widmerpool makes possible, but does not directly cause, the deaths of both men: there is a fine ambiguity about his responsibility which shows Powell at his best.) This layer is embedded in a second, a version of Powell's own wartime experience. His time with the Welch Regiment is recorded in the first two novels, and his work in Military Intelligence (Liaison) in the third. The third level is a range of literary, historical and biblical reference which is used to interpret the events of the novels; the reference to Alfred de Vigny, already quoted, is an example.

The novels' complexity arises because wartime events continually remind Nicholas of occurrences in earlier novels, and the narration halts to explain the allusions. These memories of significant earlier scenes – sugar poured over Widmerpool, for example – themselves act as comments on present events, often casting them as comic. The accumulation of names and incidents from the past, together with the meandering present-tense story, creates a disturbing lack of direction.

Powell's narration gives priority to nothing. This indicates his purpose, if not his subject: to diminish the significance usually attached to the war by making all its events appear equally comic and equally without meaning. This has obvious political consequences if the war is considered to be a time of social and political change.

His main strategy is to destroy the sense of the future. The novels render the past immense and the future negligible. There is only one significant reference to the future in the three novels. Nicholas and his wife Isobel are about to become parents:

> There was a lot to talk about . . . Instead of dealing with myriad problems in a businesslike manner, settling all kinds of points that had to be settled, making arrangements about the future – if it could be assumed that there was to be a future – we talked of more immediate, more amusing matters. (1973, p. 152)

That is all. The future can be deferred, even at the birth of a child.

Writing in the 1960s, Powell was well aware that other people had had hopes of the post-war years. Three examples from the latter part of *The Military Philosophers* show this. A sentence describing the post-Normandy advance of tanks across the Netherlands towards Germany has been well analysed by James Tucker, who sees that Powell's intention is to discourage feelings of excitement about the event, and to slow the pace of the writing. The sentence reads: 'Armour was moving in a leisurely manner across this dull flat country, designed by Nature for a battlefield, over which armies had immemorially campaigned' (1971, p. 176). Before we know it, we are in the past and any implication that present action has a bearing on the future vanishes. This is in distinct contrast to such Normandy and post-Normandy novels as Baron's *From the City, From the Plough*, Holbrook's *Flesh Wounds* or Colin MacInnes's *To the Victor the Spoils* (1950), in which the drive into Germany is part of an expression of hope for the future.

This negation of the future in favour of the past is usually executed with great skill, but a guiding hand shows through in Nicholas's reflections during the service of thanksgiving for victory at St Paul's:

> Quite soon, of course, people would, in any case begin to say the war was pointless, particularly those, and their associates, moral and actual, who had chalked on walls, 'Strike now in the West' or 'Bomb Rome'. Political activities of that kind might by now have brought together Mrs Andriadis and Gypsy Jones. (p. 231)

The general allusion is to the Left's campaign for a Second Front; the internal allusion (typically doubled) is to the left-wing politics of Gypsy Jones, with whom Nicholas had had a brief affair in the 1930s. It is difficult to grasp the point being made, however. Most people felt that Hitler had to be defeated, including the appeasers. Why the Left 'particularly' should think this is especially puzzling. A Labour government was about to come to power, and the Left was unlikely now to dismiss the war as pointless. It is difficult to resist the conclusion that Powell's right-wing views – readily apparent in his autobiography *To Keep the Ball Rolling* (1983) – have got the better of his literary detachment. Those on the Left must be denigrated: what could be more damaging than to suggest that they thought the war not worth fighting?

In the final scene of the novel Powell alludes to the belief that there should be a better post-war world, a central People's War theme. Nicholas goes to Olympia to choose his demobilization clothing, where the quantities are immense, the assistants enthusiastic: 'Was this promise of a better world? Perhaps one had reached that already and this was a celestial haberdasher's' (p. 248). The possibility is raised, and elegantly evaded. All three examples show that Powell was well aware of the People's War arguments and set out to oppose them in his fiction. Nicholas's 'emptiness', his capacity to absorb all kinds of experience, but his inability to assess or evaluate it except in terms of earlier events, is part of this opposition. So is the narrative procedure: the overall lack of narrative impetus, the reluctant forward movement, the frequent turning back – all deny that the present moment can take meaning from its projection forward into a wished-for future. These procedures amount to a political interpretation of the war – muted, oblique, a matter of implication rather than explicit statement, but political nevertheless.

Evelyn Waugh's fiction does not lack narrative impetus. His war trilogy, *The Sword of Honour*, is carefully structured in clear-cut episodes quite unlike the subtly merging scenes found in Powell. In Waugh the alert reader is able to discover significant connections, rather than being immersed in Powell's suggestive uncertainties, in which there can always be another moment of disillusion because the past is always ready to provide its deflating cross-reference. In Waugh there is a positive drive towards disillusion. At the end of each novel in the trilogy, Guy Crouchback suffers a defeat. In *Men at Arms* (1952) he is responsible for the death of Apthorpe, the novel's main comic creation. *Officers and Gentlemen* (1955) ends with his disillusion over Ivor Claire, an officer who has deserted during the battle of Crete. In *Unconditional Surrender* (1961) he is dismayed by the deaths, at the hands of Tito's Communists, of two Jews whom he has befriended.

There can be no doubt that Waugh's trilogy is intended as a criticism of the People's War concept. At the outset Guy Crouchback is pleased by the alliance between Germany and the Soviet Union because he opposes both; together they are 'the Modern Age in arms', and Guy is against the Modern Age. He is a Catholic whose values derive from history, specifically from the symbolic significance he attributes to the tomb of Sir Roger of Waybroke, an Englishman who set out for the Second Crusade but was killed in Italy, where Guy now lives. On the day of his return to England Guy goes to the tomb and touches Sir Roger's sword for luck. This is the sword of honour. ' "Sir Roger, pray for me," he said, "and for our endangered kingdom" ' (Waugh, 1984, p. 12). The sword of dishonour appears later, in 1943, when the Sword of Stalingrad is exhibited as a symbol of the relationship between Britain and the Soviet Union.

This alliance is a moral disaster, for it is dishonourable to fight beside Communism. Guy's unusual opinions mean that as the war nears what is for everyone else its successful conclusion, he becomes increasingly disillusioned. Success for the people is for Guy surrender. This was the reverse of most views of the situation. It is an assertion of a principle, of a belief in the high terms on which war should be fought. If one's ideals are set high enough, they are bound to remain unfulfilled, and by this means Waugh can contrive Guy's disillusion. However, Guy's self-dedication to the values of Sir Roger is among the very few decisive actions that he takes. Once his view of the war is established, he becomes the empty vehicle for all kinds of wartime experience.

These are comic novels about the army in which we find him surrounded by confusion and mismanagement and (no longer comically) disaster, as in Crete. He is also surrounded by the novel's villains, who are usually members of the working class: Trimmer, the skilled exploiter of others, and Ludovic, the murderer. These characterizations are a further aspect of Waugh's campaign against the People's War.

Despite the oddity of Guy's views, and Waugh's evident support for them, the *Sword of Honour* trilogy is highly regarded. It is 'probably the greatest work of fiction to emerge from the

Second World War', writes Andrew Rutherford in *The Literature of War* (1978, p. 113), and there have been other similar assessments. This judgement is probably based less on an acceptance of Guy's political views than on a recognition that Waugh writes extremely well about being in the army and, in the Cretan episode, about fighting. Waugh's trilogy improves with each succeeding volume, and for this reason I shall be devoting more attention to the final volume, *Unconditional Surrender*, than to its predecessors.

Men at Arms describes the training of officers in the Royal Halberdiers, an imaginary regiment partly based on the Royal Marines. Three important characters appear: Apthorpe, possessor of a portable toilet which is booby-trapped and explodes under him; Brigadier Ritchie-Hook, the eccentric but brave man (also responsible for the booby-trap), who returns from the Dakar raid with the head of a black man; and Virginia Troy, Guy's former wife. Neither the 'thunder-box' episode, nor the story of the head (later pickled) is particularly amusing. Apthorpe dies after Guy, behaving like a sleepwalker, provides him with a bottle of whisky in hospital.

The real purpose of the novel is to establish the importance of military values. Apthorpe may be absurd, but he is buried to 'the faultless balance of the Halberdier slow march' (p. 192). Guy may be a fool with whisky, but he deeply admires the traditions of the regiment. We meet those doubtful individuals Trimmer and Corporal-Major Ludovic. They, like Apthorpe, are unwilling to divulge their pasts. If their past lives do become known, they are invariably found to be disreputable. These are the men who have joined a regiment with honourable traditions.

Officers and Gentlemen has a lighter touch than its predecessor, is more amusing in its comic episodes and more weighty in its treatment of the war. The meeting between Trimmer and Virginia in Glasgow, which will have such important consequences for Guy, is skilfully handled. Trimmer is dressed as a Scotsman in kilt and sporran and wears major's crowns to which he is not entitled. It is a meeting typical of wartime, opportunistic on both sides. Trimmer is out of his class with Virginia, but 'It was the present moment and the next five minutes which counted with Virginia' (p. 252). (It is Guy and Ivor Claire who 'each in his way saw life *sub specie aeternitatis*', p. 259.) Virginia spends four days with Trimmer. She has no sense of the past, and therefore no principles.

In contrast to the values of this liaison, the battle in Crete is shown to have much to do with the achievement and loss of manhood. A minor character, Sarum-Smith, is described as 'not a particularly attractive man, but man he was' (p. 356). On the day of evacuation Guy 'had no clear apprehension that this was a fatal morning, that he was that day to resign an immeasurable piece of his manhood' (p. 368). The Halberdiers too are true men, for they do everything correctly; even in retreat every man is in full marching order.

The return to Egypt is a return to 'the old ambiguous world' (p. 383) of dishonour. Ivor Claire's desertion is hushed up. His guilt turns upon the fact that clear orders were given for fighting officers and men to surrender and go into captivity (this does not include Guy, who is in Intelligence). Guy has a copy of these orders in his notebook. Eventually he burns the notebook; but not until after 22 June 1941, the day of the German invasion of the Soviet Union. It is no longer possible to be honourable.

So persuasive is Waugh that it is worth recalling that Hitler's unwise invasion eventually made Allied victory possible. Waugh is asking his readers to assent to the proposition that victory should only have been achieved on honourable terms, that is, without the Communists. But people rarely have such ideals as Guy, and most, indeed, live in the 'ambiguous world' all the time. Most fiction, too, is an ordering of that ambiguous world, not the hopeful projection of an ideal. Utopian notions are a nudging presence in *Officers and Gentlemen*, though with Julia Stitch's ruthless efforts to save Ivor the novel re-enters the ambiguous world just soon enough, and with enough conviction, to prevent it appearing primarily a novel with intentions upon the reader.

Guy Crouchback's Yugoslavian experience is crucial to the success of the trilogy. His disillusionment must be conclusively demonstrated in the final volume if the pathos of his character is to carry the immense significance attached to it. Before he wrote the novel, Waugh told Frederick J. Stopp that it would concern 'Crouchback's realization that no good comes from public causes; only private causes of the soul' (quoted Rutherford, p. 130). This is what the novel, as written, can be said to show. Guy acts well in remarrying his former wife when she is pregnant by another man, but he fails when his friendship for two Jews leads to their deaths. The choices possible in personal life are superior in value to those possible in public life, and the two realms are separate from each other.

Unconditional Surrender begins in August 1943 and ends in early 1945. Guy joins Hazardous Offensive Operations. Major Ludovic inspects the Sword of Stalingrad in Westminster Abbey, and writes first his *pensées* and subsequently a novel, *Death Wish*: the wrong sword and the worthless novel with the significant title will become dominant points of reference in the novel. Virginia has become pregnant by Trimmer and Guy agrees to marry her a second time, largely, we infer, for the sake of the child. Guy then goes to Bari on the Adriatic in Italy to join 'the British Mission to the Anti-Fascist Forces of National Liberation (Adriatic)' (p. 505), by which is meant Fitzroy Maclean's 37th Military Mission to the Yugoslavs. He is flown to 'Begoy' as a military liaison officer to the Partisans. We see little of the Partisans themselves, for Guy's interest is caught by a group of displaced persons, 108 Jews whose rescue he tries to arrange. In London Virginia (now a Catholic) gives birth to a boy, puts him with friends, and is herself killed by a flying bomb. Guy is apparently not deeply troubled by the news and continues his work, but we are to understand this is one of the first of many blows to his inner nature. A propaganda demonstration of the Partisans' fighting ability is put on for an American general accompanied by Ritchie-Hook. The attack is botched and Ritchie-Hook killed. The Jews are evacuated, with the exception of the Kanyis, a married couple from an unspecified central European country, and about whom Guy had particularly cared; his attempts to help them lead to their deaths, condemned before a Partisans' People's Court. *Unconditional Surrender* proposes that in the political world betrayal and failure are invevitable, but that grace may be achieved by unselfish private acts. In demonstrating that politics are not a possible mode of being, Waugh denounces a particular kind of politics, the Communism of Tito's Partisans.

Waugh's own experience in Yugoslavia began when Randolph Churchill recruited him for Maclean's mission in June 1944. He arrived at Topusko, the Partisan headquarters in Croatia, on or just after 10 September. This was crucial to the formation of Waugh's view of the Yugoslav situation, for his months there coincided with the beginning of the rise of Soviet influence on the Partisans, and the lessening of British influence.

If Waugh's *Diaries* are read alongside Fitzroy Maclean's *Eastern Approaches* (1949), his fascinating account of the 37th Military Mission, it becomes obvious that Waugh had a limited understanding of the Partisans, of the methods of guerrilla warfare, and of recent events in Croatia. Shortly after his return in September he wrote:

> Note on Jugoslav policy: they have no interest in fighting the Germans but are engrossed in their civil war. All their vengeful motives are concentrated on the Ustashe who are reported bloodthirsty. They make slightly ingenuous attempts to deceive us into thinking their motive in various tiny campaigns is to break German retreat routes. (*Diaries*, 16 September 1944, Davie, p. 579)

The Ustače were Croat nationalists who set up a state 'on strictly Fascist lines' (Maclean, p. 270) when the Germans invaded in 1941. They *were* bloodthirsty, as Waugh well knew. The Ustače, the Chetniks under Draža Mihajlovic, and Communist-led Partisans under Tito were fighting the civil war. For the British the issue was which of the two latter groups was making the most significant military attacks on the Germans. When Maclean established that the Chetniks – formed around officers and men of the Royal Yugoslav Army – were not only not fighting very vigorously but in many cases were actively collaborating with the Germans, Allied aid, which had formerly gone to the Chetniks, was redirected to Tito's Partisans. This was Maclean's initial achievement, and the decision was made on military grounds, without regard to the long-term political outcome. Winston Churchill told the House of Commons in May 1944: 'We have declared ourselves the strong supporters of Marshal Tito because of his heroic and massive struggle against the German armies.' Waugh's assertion that the Partisans were not fighting the Germans is demonstrably untrue. Yet when the question arises in *Unconditional Surrender* of how hard the Partisans are fighting, Guy is made to say, ' "As far as I know, they aren't" ' (p. 544). It is his only remark on the subject, and carries great weight.

Waugh's remarks about 'tiny' campaigns against German retreat routes refers to 'Operation Ratweek', which took place in the first week of September, just before his return. This was conceived by Maclean, who guessed, correctly, that the Germans might be about to retreat from Greece and the Balkans to take up a more defensible position to the north. To prevent this, the most likely lines of retreat by road and rail were attacked. In a highly successful piece of co-operation between Tito and the Allies, involving Partisans, US bombers and the RAF, the operation was carried out all across the country, from Serbia to Croatia. It is local incidents in this operation that Waugh characterizes as 'various tiny campaigns'. Either he did not know what was going on, or he made no attempt to find out, or he did not care to know; that he was at Partisan headquarters a few days after 'Ratweek' took place makes his remarks all the more astonishing.

In the novel, Ritchie-Hook is killed after he attacks the fort, 'signalling fiercely, summoning to the advance the men behind him, who were already slinking away' (p. 558). Since Ritchie-Hook was not their leader and was inviting them to advance over open ground, it is difficult to blame them for disappearing. For Waugh, the incident fulfils two functions, both necessary to his wish to establish Guy's disillusion with the war. First, this is another example of the betrayals inevitable in public causes. Secondly, the incident is distressing for Guy, who admired Ritchie-Hook and has lost a mentor. In this respect it is a crucial instance of Guy's receptive 'emptiness' as a character. We are not told that he is distressed, but are left to infer his feelings. If, as readers, we then sympathize with him, we are drawn to confirm Waugh's interpretation of the war as an ever worsening series of betrayals. In this way Guy's under-defined character is the means by which the reader is persuaded to make a political interpretation of the war.

Waugh could not admit Partisan effectiveness, for the Partisans were Communists, representing in the symbolic scheme of the novel the negative values associated with the Sword of Stalingrad.

The distortions in his account of the Partisans in *Unconditional Surrender* are subtly misleading and difficult to explicate. The timing of Guy's arrival, in March 1944, is significant. Maclean had been in Yugoslavia since the previous September, and F. W. Deakin (whom Waugh admired, as he disliked Maclean) even longer, so the British had well-established relations with Tito before the Soviet mission arrived in March 1944. By arranging this coincidence of arrival, Waugh is able to include in Guy's first impressions of Begoy (Topusko) the unpleasant sensation that the Soviet mission 'lurked invisibly' in the town (p. 520), giving the impression of a sinister influence at work that was not justified by the facts. The remark 'The Russians instructed Tito . . .' (p. 535) is misleading because Maclean's account – and most others – makes it plain that Tito operated with considerable independence from Soviet influence. When Tito does go to Moscow, slipping away without telling the British mission, Waugh makes de Souza (a covert Communist) announce that 'Tito has left Vis and gone to join the Russians' (p. 560). 'Join' is ingeniously ambiguous: Tito has joined them for talks without telling the Allies, but the implication that he had irrevocably gone over to the other side is false.

Guy is briefed twice before his mission, first by an enthusiast for the Partisans, Major Cattermole – whose views perhaps resemble those of Deakin – and later by the more sceptical Brigadier Cape. Speaking of nationalism, Communism and women fighters, Cattermole uses 'we' as though British and Partisan interests are identical (p. 513). Cape says that 'some British soldiers seem to have joined up with the partisans' (p. 515), which is misleading if

taken to imply that they have left the British army, but true of
those who came to think of themselves as Partisans, which many
did. Waugh leaves the former possibility temptingly open for the
unwary reader. Cape also tells Guy that the Germans are only in
Yugoslavia to maintain communications with Greece and prevent
flanking attacks along the Adriatic coast. This would only be one
character's point of view, were it not supported by the novel's
narrative voice: 'The trunk road to the Balkans ran east. There the
German lorries streamed night and day without interruption and
the German garrisons squatted waiting the order to retire' (p.
520). As we have seen, that order came in September and was
frustrated by 'Ratweek', which is not alluded to in the novel. The
Germans made a fierce defence of Belgrade before it fell in
October, and – in one of the most peculiar incidents of the war –
German forces still in Croatia after the European cessation of
hostilities on 8 May 1945 were ordered to fight on. German
behaviour in Yugoslavia was that of an occupying power carrying
out the policies of Fascism, which included the elimination of
Jews. The situation scarcely supports the implication that the
Germans thought of Yugoslavia as being on the way to some-
where else.

Waugh makes the Partisans seem all the more irrelevant by
emphasizing the difficulties of the 108 Jews who apply to Guy for
help. Guy's concern for them is the consummation, 'in one
frustrated act of mercy' (p. 566) of his years in the army. Waugh is
preparing the final betrayal, the conclusive instance of the impos-
sibility of public good.

When the Kanyis are held back and tried by a People's Court,
Mme Kanyi is accused – as the consequence of a kindly visit by
Guy – of being the mistress of a British liaison officer. His gift of
old American magazines becomes 'American counter-revolution-
ary propaganda' (p. 568). Perhaps the Yugoslav Partisans
behaved in this way; but for most readers the whole episode is
reminiscent of Soviet trials of this kind, and takes much of its force
from that association. In view of Waugh's persistent misrepresen-
tation of the Yugoslavs, the episode should be read as a further
attempt to assimilate the Partisans to a generalized notion of

'communism' and its evils, rather than to give a specific account of
Yugoslav conditions. Guy is left with 'the sense of futility' (p.
569), and his final disillusionment. It is a further instance of the
success of the values associated with the Sword of Stalingrad.

At their last meeting Mme Kanyi summarizes the death wish
theme, which now extends from Ludovic's novel, through Guy, to
herself:

> 'Is there any place that is free from evil? It is too simple to say
> that only the Nazis wanted war. These communists wanted it
> too. It was the only way in which they could come to power.
> Many of my people wanted it, to be revenged on the Germans,
> to hasten the creation of the national state. It seems to me there
> was a will to war, a death wish, everywhere. Even good men
> thought their private honour would be satisfied by war.' (p.
> 232)

Guy admits that he too had once thought in this way. If we accept
the premises it is a moving moment in which two people with
different experiences of suffering come together in mutual recognition of its sources in European culture and politics. But what of
the premises? Yugoslavia was invaded by the Germans in April
1941. The first organized resistance was by the Chetniks in May,
and the Communists did not join in until July, after and probably
as a consequence of the German invasion of the Soviet Union in
June. That summer, Partisans and Chetniks fought together, but
the Partisans eventually won the civil war because they were
successful in fighting the Germans. This puts Mme Kanyi's speech
in rather a different perspective from that intended by Waugh.
Events were complex and unpredictable, and there was nothing
inevitable about Communist success. The Chetniks chose to be
inactive or collaborate because they hoped to achieve power after
a German victory. It was both sides, not one, who wanted power;
and every group thinking of itself as nationalist (except the
outright collaborators) wanted to revenge themselves on the
Germans. There were all kinds of nationalism, whether Croatian,
Serbian or Yugoslav; Tito's break with Stalin in 1948 was a claim

for national independence. The politics of Mme Kanyi's fine speech do not stand up to examination.

When Mme Kanyi speaks of 'my people' wanting war, she apparently refers to all Jews, for she is herself from a central European state, speaks only German and Italian, and is not a Yugoslav. Waugh requires her moral authority as a displaced Jew to deliver the most effective possible retort to Communism. If 'the national state' refers to the setting up of Israel in 1948, Mme Kanyi is saying – or Waugh is arguing – that the European Jews 'wanted' an anti-Semitic war to be conducted against themselves in order to make Israel possible. If this is so, the novel's death wish theme has been radically over-extended into an area of political interpretation where Waugh cannot possibly be followed.

The notion of a universal death wish is in any case very difficult to accept. Waugh introduces Mme Kanyi's speech in order to make it seem more plausible; an endorsement from a Jewish source is beyond criticism. The difficulties of the one hundred and eight Jews have already pushed the Partisans out of the central position they might have been expected to occupy in the novel. Our knowledge of the Jews' historical situation and their persecution predisposes us to assent to this. But when Waugh brings in the Partisans' People's Court to condemn the Kanyis, and so complete the structural and emotional requirements of the *Sword of Honour* trilogy by ensuring Guy's utter disillusion, we may feel that our sympathies for the Kanyis have been improperly invoked in order to achieve our assent to what Waugh has set out to 'prove': that there can be no good in public causes, only in private ones.

It must be apparent that I find the politics of *Unconditional Surrender* to be an insufficient justification for Guy's disillusion with the war. The novel is often described as being extremely well written and carefully and effectively structured. This is undoubtedly true; it gives pleasure. Perhaps we should think of it – and the trilogy as a whole – as being like a story first heard in childhood, a fantasy that never loses its charm, but which it would be fatal to live by.

Waugh no longer has the subject of Yugoslavia to himself, for

Thomas Keneally's *Season in Purgatory* (1976) tells the story of British doctors attached to the Partisans. A new arrival describes his departure from Bari:

> 'They have a quite famous officer there, waiting to be parachuted into Yugoslavia. Famous novelist. Evelyn Waugh. Very snooty. Hard man to deal with. Quick wit. Couldn't understand half his allusions.' (p .164)

Season in Purgatory may be read as a reply to *Unconditional Surrender*. It is at least as well structured and as well written as Waugh's novel. It is largely episodic, and describes the experiences of Captain David Pelham among the Partisans, first on the mainland and then on the offshore islands. It is a novel of political education, and shows a remarkable skill in describing the emotions felt in political situations. Keneally's research draws on Maclean's *Eastern Approaches*, but one of his primary sources is *Guerilla Surgeon* by Lindsay Rogers, a New Zealander who worked in Partisan hospitals from autumn 1943 until early 1945. He became an admirer of Partisan courage and fighting ability, and though he was not a Communist shared their hopes for a better future. Rogers valued most the uncomplicated commitment of 1943, 'the good old days of 1943, when offensive action and guerilla warfare were the whole of the struggle' (Rogers, 1957, p. 246).

Keneally's novel is set during this heroic period, and the question of dating is again important. Captain David Pelham's purgatory runs from September 1943 to June 1944, so that it is completed before relations between Tito and the Allies began to deteriorate in September. Pelham treats appalling and unusual injuries in difficult circumstances and with incomplete medical supplies, driving himself to exhaustion and collapse. He has shown a commitment to the Partisans that begins with his professional skills as a surgeon and ends as something more profound, a humanist belief in the value of what the Partisans are doing that contrasts starkly with the depressed uninterest of Guy Crouchback.

For Waugh 'being a Partisan' is impossible, a joke; but Lindsay

Rogers is a little too eager to enrol himself as one, and his attitude too forthright for ready transposition into fiction. In this situation Keneally makes Pelham's Partisan identity emerge indirectly. British, upper middle class and an Anglo-Catholic, he is not an obvious candidate. He becomes a pacifist when a captured German dies on his operating table:

> In his bloodstream were two simple propositions: that the savagery of the Germans did not excuse the savagery of the partisans: that the savagery of the partisans did not excuse the savagery of the Germans. That the masters of the ideologies, even the bland ideology of democracy, were blood-crazed. That at the core of their political fervour, there stood a desire to punish with death anyone who hankered for other systems than those approved. (p. 178)

In Waugh the death wish is universal, but here it is located in the minds and actions of men of power. Pelham's work is to resist death through surgery, whereas Guy's detachment from his work is an aspect of the death wish, destructively internalized. Pelham's war makes him desire change in the future, so that after the war he joins CND; Guy's war makes him long for immediate extinction.

Public and private attitudes towards a politicized sexuality merge during one of the most distressing episodes in the novel, Pelham's distant glimpse of Partisan women fighting:

> They were moving fast up through the vineyards, taking big steps. They began falling. It was all so noiseless at binocular-distance that David thought they were merely tripping on the steep earth. In fifteen seconds one in three fell down. Soon, it seemed, one in two. He did not want to see how the event ended. He gave the glasses back to the officer, who was still shrugging off imaginary flies.
>
> 'Who,' demanded the young officer, 'said that women are only good for housework?'
>
> From the insane question Pelham stumbled to his rest in the barn. (p. 207)

The distancing and the refusal to go on watching are both correct strategies. Keneally cannot legitimately claim, for himself or for his character Pelham, any inwardness with women who can fight like this. To do so would require an impossible dissolution of subjective identity, whether by the author, his character or the reader. A political understanding of what these women are doing is perfectly possible, if far from adequate to such a way of dying. It was not the first time, wrote Frank Thompson in 1941, that the Slavs 'have thrown their bodies between Europe and destruction. They bore the brunt of the Turks and Tartars too. "To suffer like a Slav" will soon become a by-word in all the world's languages' (Thompson and Thompson, 1947, p. 38). That phrase has never become proverbial. Silence – of a kind broken by *Season in Purgatory* – and indifference – of a kind embodied in *Unconditional Surrender* – have ensured that.

C. P. Snow's eleven-volume *Strangers and Brothers* sequence (1949–70) devotes two novels to the war years. *The New Men*, published in 1954, covers the period 1939–47, and has as its subject the British contribution to the development of the atomic bomb. *Homecomings* (1956), overlaps with it, covering the years 1938–51, and is primarily concerned with Lewis Eliot's private life, particularly the suicide of Sheila, his first wife, and the relationship with his second, Margaret Davidson.

Early in the war many academics with specialist abilities joined government ministries as temporary senior civil servants. Lewis Eliot is shown making this characteristic move into new work. He learns of the atom bomb project at an early stage, and is drawn into it further when his brother Martin joins the research team at 'Barford'. Walter Luke, a scientist from Eliot's own Cambridge college, is a leading member of the team: these are the 'new men' whose lives combine science and politics. Eventually the moral implications of their research begin to trouble some of the scientists, and Martin drafts a letter to the press protesting at British involvement with the use of the bomb at Hiroshima. Lewis, who largely agrees with him, nevertheless persuades him to do nothing, in order to preserve his career. When it becomes known that one of the scientific team is passing information to the Soviet Union, Lewis is again consulted and again gives advice as an official which differs from his personal feelings. Both incidents show Snow's concern with the conflict between private belief and the politics of public life.

In *Homecomings* Lewis's future wife is twelve years younger than he, an outgoing 'woman of character' with an energy and a sense of her own identity sufficient to disturb Lewis's friend Roy Calvert. Margaret is not a *femme fatale* (as Virginia Troy and Pamela Flitton are), but she is vivid where Lewis is indistinct; his advantage over her is that through his job he has access to power. This becomes a factor in their relationship. 'The official world, the corridors of power, the dilemmas of conscience and egotism – she disliked them all' (Snow, 1984, p. 591). Margaret leaves Eliot to marry a doctor whose life is not 'full of the steady, confident voices of power' (p. 612). She returns to him when he can tell her that he is 'not held any longer by the chessboard of power' (p. 674). Love and companionship, the conclusion of the narrative tells us, triumph over the enjoyment of power.

However, if we attend to the middle of this lengthy novel, rather than to its ending, its subject appears rather differently. *Strangers and Brothers* is a frigid epic, a history of self-restraint in the pursuit of success. The two war novels in the sequence have a double subject, Lewis Eliot's education into feeling and his work as a civil servant. Each theme is the expression of a form of desire. Success in love leads to erotic 'abandonment', whilst success at the ministry gives Eliot the opportunity to exercise power. The main drives of the novel are therefore complementary, and not contradictory as some critics have believed. Yet each drive has to act against considerable resistance. For Eliot, the expression of emotion is close to being an act of will. He cannot tell Margaret that his first wife killed herself, and he does not anticipate the distress caused by this suppression and its inevitable revelation.

Coldness is everywhere. Lewis thinks of Sheila as one of those who are 'locked in their own coldness' (p. 502). In the argument between the two brothers towards the end of *The New Men* each reproaches the other with being cold: 'I said that he was so self-centred that no human being mattered to him . . . He had been a failure so long that he had not a glimmer of warmth left' (p. 458). Martin, hoping to oppose the consequences of making the bomb from outside the system rather than from within it, justifies himself with the remark that ' "Sometimes it's only the cold who can be useful" ' (p. 476).

These instances of coldness are thematic and deliberate. When the same coolness enters the novel's treatment of sexuality, it may not be intentional. In *The New Men* Eliot is made to speak clumsily of the close relationship between death and the erotic:

> I could not recall of those who had known more than their share of the erotic life, one who, when the end came, did not think that his time had been tolerably well spent. (p. 434)

Perhaps this mimics Eliot's self-restraint; taking a 'share' in the limited supply of erotic experience has to be justified. But nowhere in the novels does Snow find an appropriate language to convey erotic love. This is a post-coital Eliot in bed with Margaret: 'She was relaxed because I was happy, just as I had seen her abandoned because she was giving me pleasure' (p. 572). The woman loses herself so that Eliot may be conscious of his own pleasure; their mutual eroticism is obliterated by his egotism.

A difficult passage occurs in Lewis's account of sexual experience in his marriage to Sheila:

> Although it was rarely that I had her – (as our marriage went on, it was false to speak of making love, for about it there was, though she did not often refuse me, the one-sidedness of rape) – nevertheless she was easier if I slept in the same room. (p. 516)

This passage does not have the coarse violence of Powell's Duport speaking of Pamela Flitton ('I only stuffed her once'), but Lewis – and perhaps Snow too – seems unaware of the hardness of that 'had'. Is the reference to rape self-critical? Does Lewis recognize that the assertion of his marital rights is little short of an attack on Sheila, whom he knows to be depressed and increasingly mentally ill? The uncertainty arises because Lewis Eliot is another 'empty' figure, the passive vehicle for all kinds of experience, not all of it clearly judged.

Politically Snow is committed to the future. *The New Men* is intended to be a contribution to the debate taking place during the 1950s over the possession and use of nuclear weapons. It recuperates the debates of the war and immediate post-war years in order to make them available as a basis of understanding for concerned readers. This explains one of the peculiarities of Snow's war novels: that the ordinary experience of war scarcely appears in them. Bombs do not fall, telephones always work, trains are not interrupted, nobody (except Roy Calvert, who is in Bomber Command) is killed. The People's War is suppressed in order to clarify a debate about responsibility for the atom bomb. The unusual periodization of *The New Men* – 1939 to 1947 – indicates that the war years are being interpreted as leading, not towards victory in 1945, but towards the inauguration in that year of a post-Hiroshima world through which we are still living. Snow's is a fiction of public responsibility. This is also apparent, less admirably, in his evident pleasure in the processes of power, signified in the novels by Hector Rose, the permanent secretary at the ministry. This pleasure in power contrasts with the unpleasurable writing about sex. Snow raises the question of the nature of desire but is unable to find a language to describe erotic experience; and he is a political liberal attracted by the exercise of power to the extent that his novels legitimize bureaucratic processes. He succeeds, however, in showing how the development of nuclear weapons originated the greatest moral and political issue of our own time. Among the novels discussed here, his are exceptional in finding the meaning of the war years in their orientation towards the future.

The interest of Olivia Manning's *Balkan Trilogy* arises from its unusual perspective upon the war. The first two volumes are set in Bucharest and the third in Athens. Harriet and Guy Pringle are forced to move twice, first when the Germans occupy Romania in October 1940, and again when Greece is invaded in April 1941. Experience of the preliminaries to invasion and occupation is

necessarily unusual in English fiction. The history of the war in the
Balkans produces an unfamiliar periodization of the novels. The
first, *The Great Fortune* (1960) begins just before the outbreak of
war in 1939 and concludes with news of the fall of Paris on 13
June 1940. This conventional periodization – it also occurs in
Powell's *The Valley of Bones* – is strengthened by tying in Guy's
production of *Troilus and Cressida*: Troy and Paris fall together.
The second volume, *The Spoilt City* (1962), runs from June to
October 1940, when Harriet flies out of Romania, arriving in
Greece without Guy. Shortly before her departure there is a raid
on the Pringles' flat and Sasha Drucker, a young Jew whom they
have been concealing, is taken away by members of the Iron
Guard, the Romanian Fascist party. *Friends and Heroes* (1965)
completes the trilogy, and includes many reflections upon Harriet's difficulties with her husband Guy, her relationship with
Charles Warden, and the death of Prince Yakimov, an amusing
sponger. It ends with the disorganized departure of the British
community for Egypt.

Although these novels benefit from their unusual settings, they
also domesticate the experience of war by centring attention upon
the strange relationship between Harriet and Guy, who have been
married for only a few weeks when the first novel opens. The
action takes place in the flats, parks, bars, restaurants, hotels and
offices of Budapest and Athens. It is in this semi-public world that
Harriet tries to discover Guy and establish her marriage. Guy is
politically on the Left, she is not; Guy is gregarious, she is more
cautious and consequently lonely. The trilogy is a critique of
Guy's politics and behaviour, from Harriet's point of view.

Although it ends with the conventional assertion that 'they
were together and would remain together' (Manning, 1981, p.
924), the ending is untrue to the problems of the marriage. Guy is
always busy. He teaches literature at the university (for a thinly
disguised British Council), he produces plays and revues; he
knows dozens, perhaps hundreds of people, helping many with
money and with sympathy. All are more important to him than
his wife, whom he ignores. He defends himself in terms that are at
once absurd and disturbing:

Having married her, he simply ceased to see her as another person. She had once accused him of considering her feelings less than those of anyone else with whom they came into contact. Surprised, he had said: 'But you are myself. I don't need to consider your feelings.' (p. 765)

This astonishing reply values marriage, and Harriet, at the same time as it leaves space for Guy to act destructively towards her, breaking the threads between them. From the outset, Harriet is attracted towards other men, towards Clarence Lawson in the first volume and – more seriously – towards Charles Warden in the third. The latter relationship is about to be consummated in a hotel bedroom in Athens when the abducted Sasha reappears and the moment is lost. This interruption is peculiarly opportune, for it prevents Harriet acting significantly outside the marriage. She never commits herself with anyone else. ' "Charles loved me," ' she tells Guy (p. 876), but she does not describe her own feelings.

In *The Balkan Trilogy* Harriet discovers that Guy is difficult because he wishes to preserve his own freedom: that is why he makes so many friends and yet so few commitments. (Harriet makes few friends and few commitments.) She, who sees herself as 'an equal and a comrade' (p. 548), feels that 'his attitude betrayed the concept of mutual defence which existed in marriage' (p. 764), and that this betrayal gives her 'just cause for revolt' (p. 786). Yet this revolt ends in submission, and it is the timidity of her objections to Guy that makes it difficult to find in Harriet's dissatisfactions a woman significantly defining herself against masculine power. These are Harriet's reflections upon encountering Guy's colleague and friend Ben Phipps:

He had about him the reek of the trouble-maker, the natural enemy of married life; the sort of man who observes, or seems to observe, the conventions while leading husbands astray and undermining the authority of wives. (p. 713)

Harriet's revolt is an emotionally conservative one, in favour of marriage as a defensive union against the outside world. Guy, who wishes to be open to the outside world, is quite different from her, but she reflects that 'perhaps, unawares, it was his difference she had married' (p. 755).

It is Harriet's continual probing of the meaning of Guy that sustains the trilogy. However badly he behaves he remains endlessly fascinating to her. The interest lies in the continual regeneration of Harriet's incomprehension. There is little forward narrative movement, little 'plot', and it is the passage of time that eventually forces an unconvincing resolution. 'They had learnt each other's faults and weaknesses' we are told just before the departure for Egypt, but neither character is shown to be altered by that knowledge. Guy does not change at all, and Harriet learns only that she has married an enigma. The trilogy is not as static as Powell's work, but belongs in the same category. The passing show of life in Romania and Greece may persuade unwary readers that some progress in understanding has occurred, but it has not: the Pringles have simply taken the same unresolvable problem from one country to another. As Guy says, theirs has been 'a marriage in war, and the war had not ended yet', so they must go on together, whatever their immediate problems, as long as does the war itself. 'She had chosen to make her life with Guy and would stand by her choice' (p. 897). A break is not possible. That is why Manning cannot allow anything so decisive as adultery to interfere with the perturbed progress of this marriage.

The enormous number of meals consumed in *The Balkan Trilogy* provides the opportunity for political discussion and for the development of the novels' second theme, Harriet's political criticism of Guy. It is well known that Harriet is largely based upon Olivia Manning herself, and that Guy is a version of her husband R. D. (Reggie) Smith, whom she married in the circumstances described in the novels, he being a minor official employed by the British Council in Bucharest. Reggie Smith was a member of the Communist Party before the war and remained committed throughout his life to left-wing politics. Olivia Manning herself became increasingly right wing as the years passed. Guy's political attitudes are those of the 1930s Left, but the criticism to which they are subjected is made from a position on the Right developed some twenty years later. When Guy asks Harriet why she is not a

'Progressive' she replies: ' "Truth is more complex than politics" ' (p. 718). That is a crucial remark intended to contrast his limitations with her breadth of outlook.

The criticism begins early in the first volume. At a dinner party with the Druckers, a prosperous Jewish family with business links in Germany, Guy's pro-Soviet attitude causes alarm:

> He said suddenly: 'When the Russians come here, there will be no more persecution. The Jews will be free to follow any profession they choose.'
>
> At these words, intended to comfort, the brothers-in-law turned on him faces so appalled that Harriet laughed in spite of herself (p. 103)

Guy is shown to be completely pro-Soviet, unperturbed by the German—Soviet pact and the invasion of Finland, and looking forward, like his friends, to Russian control of Romania (p. 569). Guy represents the sense of the future, but one that is compromised, from the post-war point of view, by its allegiance to Stalin, though at the time it would have had widespread popular support. Harriet's critical eye is constantly on him and his left-wing companions. 'Seeing them hold to political mysteries as other men held to God, she told herself they were . . . hopeless romantics. Their conversation did not relate to reality. She was bored' (p. 787). Harriet sees Anthony Eden, the British Foreign Secretary, at the Parthenon. She is 'transported as though some part of England itself had come to be with them' (p. 788), for which Guy considers her, too, to be a romantic. Balancing of this kind between opposed political attitudes is carefully sustained throughout the trilogy.

In the spirit of political balance, Harriet is given one sustained opportunity to develop her own politics against Guy's Marxism. She is interested by an Iron Guard pamphlet saying that Codreanu, their assassinated leader, had been killed on the instructions of King Carol. Her response is a mixture of detachment and acceptance:

> Her imagination excited by this romance of a young leader murdered by a jealous King, she thought of the men who had

handed it to her in the square. Bare-headed and dark-skinned, wearing singlets or cheap shirts without collars, they may have been artisans . . . Guy, seeing the Guardist groups pushing through the streets, had said: 'How rapidly they are gathering in their kind: the hopeless, the inadequate, the brute.' And yet, she thought, they were the only people in this spoilt city whose ideals rose above money, food and sex. Why should the brute not be infused with ideals, the hopeless given hope, the inadequate strength? (pp. 389–90)

The Iron Guard was an influential Romanian political party, usually described as Fascist. It was also known as the 'All-for-the-Fatherland' party, which Manning does not mention, though she gives its more romantic name, the Legion of the Archangel Michael. Its policy was anti-Semitic and pro-Axis (Codreanu, quoted in *Keesing's Contemporary Archives*, 29 November 1937). It threatened and carried out assassinations, and made attacks on Jews. Partly under its influence less extreme right-wing politicians introduced a number of anti-Semitic laws during 1937–40. Its leader, Zelea Codreanu, had been sentenced to ten years' imprisonment in May 1938 for activities against the state including treason. On 30 November, Codreanu, aged thirty-eight, and thirteen other members of the movement were reported to have been shot by their guards while 'attempting to escape'.

It is possible to accept Harriet's interest in this organization as part of the debate, personal as much as political, between the Pringles. The Iron Guard are working people, and they have ideals rather similar (Harriet thinks) to those of the Marxists. But Manning's deeper purpose becomes apparent when Harriet is shown discussing Codreanu with Sasha Drucker, the Jewish youth whom they have concealed in their flat:

She spoke of Codreanu, saying: 'He loved the peasants. He gave them this idea of a nation united in brotherhood. Surely the important thing was that people believed in him?'

Sasha listened uneasily. 'But he did terrible things,' he said. 'He started the pogroms [of 1937–8]. My cousin at the University was thrown out of a window. His spine was broken.'

That was the reality, of course. 'But why did the reality have to be that?' she said. The ideals had been fine enough . . . Why then, she wanted to know, must they degenerate into a reality of blackmail, persecution and murder? (p. 392)

Presented with Sasha's counter-argument that the Iron Guard has grown through the credulity of ignorant Romanian peasants, Harriet reflects that 'Wonders were born of ignorance and super-stition. Do away with ignorance and superstition and there would be no more wonders' – only the arid materialism of Guy's politics (p. 394).

Manning insists upon giving prominence to Harriet's feelings about Codreanu in order to set up a contrast between the spiritual and materialist impulses in politics. Harriet is stimulated by the 'mystical strain' (p. 390) in these Romanian Fascists, and she feels sympathy for Sasha because, like her, he 'related life to eternity rather than to time'. The philosophical materialism in which Guy's politics are grounded is the opposite of such mysticism. He lives in time and in history, rejects fantasy and looks forward to a changed future. Harriet feels 'gagged' (p. 392) by his outlook. The long perspectives in which she views events drain them of their immediate political significance, and free her to find meaning in the wide open spaces of the unattached spirit.

The two forces, Harriet and Guy, are kept in balance; Harriet has almost exclusive possession of the narrative point of view and is engagingly sharp and perceptive, but Guy is more intriguing, always politically and personally sympathetic, and an enigma that the reader, as much as Harriet, would like to understand. This equivalence should not distract us from the conservatism of Manning's position. No other politics would for a moment tolerate a sympathetic consideration of Romanian Fascism. The notion of a 'balance' between that and a then-popular form of Marxism is itself dubious: how does one take a balanced position when Hitler and his Balkan enthusiasts are on one side of the scales?

Manning uses the same strategy as does Waugh when she implicates a Jew in her political views. Waugh uses Mme Kanyi to legitimize the universal 'death wish', and Manning uses Harriet's sympathy with Sasha to make acceptable the mysticism that he is supposed to share with the Iron Guard. Nevertheless the remainder of the debate between Harriet and Guy is even-handed, and inclines to the Left in the discussions of Romanian history. Harriet's last-page abandonment of any revolt against Guy ('They were together and would remain together') unites the Pringles for reasons of narrative convenience, but it is not reconcilable with the deep emotional and political differences between them.

These differences break out again in *The Levant Trilogy*, where less effort is made to sustain the balance and the advantage tilts in favour of Harriet. The concentration on Harriet and Guy is less intense than in the earlier trilogy, but their initial problems are the same. Guy becomes Director of the Institute, and Harriet has a clerical job. Guy always has a role in Cairo, Harriet almost never. She remarks to a friend: ' "I wish I were a man fighting in the desert" ' (Manning, 1982, p. 286). She is thin and ill: 'The killing element was not the heat of Cairo but Guy himself' (p. 374). Harriet's criticism of Guy is not only more explicit here than in *The Balkan Trilogy*, it is also more personal and less political. (The one major political incident occurs when Guy employs two Jewish teachers who vanish after Professor Lord Pinkrose is shot when about to give a lecture. Guy is made to look politically naïve, particularly as he supports the Jewish cause against the British.)

There is a break between the two trilogies. The Pringles arrive in Egypt in April 1941, but *The Danger Tree* (1977) does not resume until over a year later. It opens in June 1942 with the arrival in Egypt of a new character, Simon Boulderstone, an inexperienced lieutenant whose desert war is presented in alternation with the Pringles' lives in Cairo. The stasis of their lives contrasts with Simon's moral education. The second novel, *The Battle Lost and Won* (1978), begins with Simon coming to terms with his brother's death, and ends in December 1942 with the supposed departure of Harriet for England on a ship that is subsequently sunk. *The Sum of Things* was published in 1980 (the year of Olivia Manning's death). Harriet, refusing to join the ship, has been driven to Damascus. The novel traces her months there and in Jerusalem, until she is reunited with Guy in July 1943. The novel ends in October with the departure of Simon for the Greek islands. The Pringles see him off, and Guy asks Harriet for an assurance that she will never leave him again. ' "Don't know, Can't promise." Harriet laughed and squeezed his arm: "Probably not" ' (p. 568). The commitment is marginally less absolute than it was at the end of *The Balkan Trilogy*, but nothing has changed.

In the earlier trilogy Harriet is interrupted before she can make love to Charles Warden. In the later one, variations on this theme occur. She meets an actor, Aidan Crawley, but he loves Guy, not her. In the Levant, Harriet develops an uncharacteristic timidity towards other men which removes any likelihood of her being unfaithful to Guy. Guy himself shows no interest in women after Harriet's supposed death, and begins to feel that 'the only permanent relationship was the relationship of marriage, if death or divorce did not end it' (p. 471). With both principal characters acting and feeling in this way it is scarcely surprising that upon Harriet's reappearance in Cairo the marriage should resume exactly as it was before. The narrative is never allowed to develop in such a way as to allow either Harriet or Guy to make strong extramarital relationships. This contrivance carries with it a conservative message about the necessary continuity of marriage, and the passivity of women. However badly Guy behaves towards Harriet she will never try to find an emotional life elsewhere, and – for all her sharpness – will never assert herself against him in any way that could threaten their union.

In both trilogies there are numerous references to sexual relationships between characters other than Harriet and Guy, but only one account of a sexual act. Harriet overhears Edwina in the next room:

Peter Lisdoonvarna, with joking gruffness, was telling her to 'shut up'. The sobbing grew louder and gave rise to a slap and scuffle, and Peter's voice, contused with sexual intent, spoke hoarsely: 'Come on, you little bitch. Turn over.'

Harriet pushed her bedside chair so it crashed against the door, but the noise did not interrupt the lovers who, with squeaks, grunts and a rhythmic clicking of the bed, were locked together until Peter gave out a final groan and there was an interval of quiet. (p. 322)

This defines sex as distasteful and, for Harriet, disturbing. It is a form of male aggression welcomed by the sobbing (why?) but eager woman. In the post-war epics discussed here, sexual relations have often been shown as aggression by one partner upon another, and this instance is consistent with that theme. Harriet's attempt to stop the lovers draws attention to the existence of another, subterranean, theme. Nowhere is there any mention of sexual activity between Harriet and Guy: at most, the couple touch or embrace. Immediately after overhearing the two lovers Harriet goes to hospital, thankful that someone will be responsible for 'her tired and constantly ailing body' (p. 324). There, she tells herself: ' "I want more love than I am given – but where am I to find it?" ' (p. 334). This sequence suggests that Harriet is ill because she is unloved. The expression of desire is absent from the trilogies (only Aidan's longing for Guy comes remotely close). It is extraordinary that there is no attempt to explore the sexual aspect of the Pringles' marriage. In *Middlemarch* George Eliot finds ways to suggest Casaubon's sexual failure, but Manning has less to say about desire in marriage than many novelists of the nineteenth century. The theme of unexpressed desire must be added to the political theme and the problem of Guy's behaviour as the novels' subject.

Olivia Manning's trilogies belong to the conventional novel of manners, made significant by the proximity of war. As a sustained attempt to validate an emotional and political conservatism they are a fitting summary to the generally repressive interpretation of the war made by post-war epic fiction.

Bibliography

Where two dates of publication are given for works quoted in the text, the second refers to the edition from which the quotation is taken.

FICTION

Aldridge, James, *Of Many Men*, Michael Joseph, 1946; Mayflower-Dell, 1964
– *The Sea Eagle*, Michael Joseph, 1944
Balchin, Nigel, *Mine Own Executioner*, William Collins, 1945
Ballard, J. G., *Empire of the Sun*, Victor Gollancz, 1984
Baron, Alexander, *From the City, From the Plough*, Jonathan Cape, 1948; Triad Mayflower, 1979
– *There's No Home*, Jonathan Cape, 1951
Bates, H. E., *Fair Stood the Wind for France*, Michael Joseph, 1944; Penguin, 1958
Billany, Dan, *The Trap*, Faber and Faber, 1950; reprinted 1986
Billany, Dan, and David Dowie, *The Cage*, Longmans, Green, 1949
Bowen, Elizabeth, *The Heat of the Day*, Jonathan Cape, 1949
Carr, J. L., *A Season in Sinji*, Alan Ross, 1967; Penguin, 1985
Comfort, Alex, *No Such Liberty*, Chapman and Hall, 1941
– *The Power House*, George Routledge, 1944
Dahl, Roald, *Over to You*, Penguin, 1973
Davin, Dan (ed.), *Short Stories from the Second World War*, Oxford, 1982
Deighton, Len, *SS–GB: Nazi-occupied Britain 1941*, Jonathan Cape, 1978; Triad Grafton, 1980
– *Goodbye, Mickey Mouse*, Hutchinson, 1982
– *Bomber*, Jonathan Cape, 1970
Duffy, Maureen, *Change*, Methuen, 1987
Duras, Marguerite, *La Douleur*, POL, 1985; William Collins, 1986 (trans. under same title)
Farrell, J. G., *The Singapore Grip*, Weidenfeld and Nicolson, 1978; Fontana, 1979

Green, Henry, *Caught*, Hogarth Press, 1943

Greene, Graham, 'Men at Work' in *Twenty-One Stories*, Penguin, 1970; reprinted 1977

Hamilton, Patrick, *Hangover Square*, Constable, 1941; Penguin, 1974
– *The Slaves of Solitude*, Constable, 1947

Hanley, James, *No Directions*, Faber and Faber, 1943

Harris, John, *Ride Out the Storm: A Novel of Dunkirk*, Hutchinson, 1975; Arrow, 1976

Holbrook, David, *Flesh Wounds*, Methuen, 1966; ed. G. Halson, Longmans, 1968

Hood, Stuart, *Since the Fall*, Weidenfeld and Nicolson, 1955
– *The Circle of the Minotaur*, Routledge and Kegan Paul, 1950

Keneally, Thomas, *Season in Purgatory*, William Collins, 1976

Lehmann, John (ed.), *Folios of New Writing*, Hogarth Press, 1940–1
– *New Writing and Daylight*, Hogarth Press, 1942–6

Lewis, Alun, *The Last Inspection*, Allen and Unwin, 1942

Lindsay, Jack, *Beyond Terror: A Novel of the Battle of Crete*, Andrew Dakers, 1943

Lively, Penelope, *Moon Tiger*, André Deutsch, 1987

MacInnes, Colin, *To the Victor the Spoils*, MacGibbon and Kee, 1950; Allison and Busby, 1986

Manning, Olivia, *The Balkan Trilogy*, Penguin, 1981; comprising *The Great Fortune*, Heinemann, 1960; *The Spoilt City*, Heinemann, 1962; *Friends and Heroes*, Heinemann, 1965
– *The Levant Trilogy*, Penguin, 1982; comprising *The Danger Tree*, Weidenfeld and Nicolson, 1977; *The Battle Lost and Won*, Weidenfeld and Nicolson, 1978; *The Sum of Things*, Weidenfeld and Nicolson, 1980

Monsarrat, Nicholas, *The Cruel Sea*, Cassell, 1951
– *Three Corvettes*, Cassell, 1945; Pan, 1987
– *'H.M.S. Marlborough Will Enter Harbour'*, Pan, 1987; first published as *Depends What You Mean by Love*, Cassell, 1947

Piper, David, *Trial by Battle*, William Collins, 1966; first published as written by Peter Towry, 1959

Powell, Anthony, *The Valley of Bones*, Heinemann, 1964; Fontana 1973
– *The Soldier's Art*, Heinemann, 1966; Fontana 1968
– *The Military Philosophers*, Heinemann, 1968; Fontana, 1971

Priestley, J. B., *Black-Out in Gretley*, Heinemann, 1942
– *Daylight on Saturday: A Novel About An Aircraft Factory*, Heinemann, 1943

– *Three Men in New Suits*, Heinemann, 1945; Allison and Busby, 1984

Robinson, Derek, *Kramer's War*, Hamish Hamilton, 1977

– *Piece of Cake*, Hamish Hamilton, 1983; Pan, 1984

Sansom, William, *Fireman Flower and Other Stories*, Hogarth Press, 1944

Shute, Nevil, *Landfall*, Heinemann, 1940; Pan, 1962

Snow, C. P., *Strangers and Brothers*, vol. 2, Macmillan, 1972; Penguin, 1984; including *The New Men*, Macmillan, 1954; *Homecomings*, Macmillan, 1956

Strachey, John, *Post D*, Victor Gollancz, 1941

Thomas, Leslie, *The Magic Army*, Eyre Methuen, 1981

Tressell, Robert, *The Ragged-Trousered Philanthropists*, abridged edn. 1914, full text Lawrence and Wishart 1955; Panther/Grafton, 1965

Vercors, *Le Silence de la mer*, Les Cahiers du silence, 1943; trans. as *Put Out the Light*, Macmillan, 1944

Warner, Rex, *The Aerodrome*, Bodley Head, 1941; Oxford, 1982

Waugh, Evelyn, *Put Out More Flags*, Chapman and Hall, 1942; Penguin, 1943

– *The Sword of Honour Trilogy*, Penguin, 1984; comprising *Men at Arms*, Chapman and Hall, 1952; *Officers and Gentlemen*, Chapman and Hall, 1955; *Unconditional Surrender*, Chapman and Hall, 1961

AUTOBIOGRAPHY, LETTERS, DIARIES

Buster, Gun, *Return via Dunkirk*, Hodder and Stoughton, 1940; reprinted 1975

Colville, John, *The Fringes of Power: Downing Street Diaries 1939–1955: Volume One: September 1939–September 1941*, Hodder and Stoughton, 1985; Sceptre, 1986

Dahl, Roald, *Going Solo*, Jonathan Cape, 1986; Penguin, 1987

Davidson, Basil, *Special Operations Europe: Scenes from the Anti-Nazi War*, Victor Gollancz, 1980; Grafton, 1987

Davie, Michael (ed.), *The Diaries of Evelyn Waugh*, Weidenfeld and Nicolson, 1976; Penguin, 1979

Douglas, Keith, *Keith Douglas: A Prose Miscellany*, ed. Desmond Graham, Carcanet, 1985

Hillary, Richard, *The Last Enemy*, Macmillan, 1943

Hood, Stuart, *Pebbles from My Skull*, Hutchinson, 1963

– *Carlino*, Carcanet, 1985 (reprints *Pebbles from my Skull* with Afterword)

Isherwood, Christopher, *Christopher and his Kind: 1929–1939*, Eyre Methuen, 1977

Last, Nella, *Nella Last's War: A Mother's Diary 1939–45*, ed. Richard Broad and Suzie Fleming, Falling Wall Press, 1981; Sphere, 1983

MacHorton, Ian, *Safer Than a Known Way*, Odhams, 1958; Fontana, 1975

Maclean, Fitzroy, *Eastern Approaches*, Jonathan Cape, 1949; Macmillan, 1982

Milligan, Spike, *Mussolini: His Part in My Downfall*, Michael Joseph, 1978; Penguin, 1980 (vol. 4 of war memoirs)

— *Where Have All the Bullets Gone?*, M. and J. Hobbs and Michael Joseph, 1985; Penguin 1986 (vol. 5 of war memoirs)

Mitchison, Naomi, *Among You Taking Notes . . . The Wartime Diary of Naomi Mitchison 1939–1945*, ed. Dorothy Sheridan, Victor Gollancz, 1985; Oxford 1986

Newby, Eric, *Love and War in the Apennines*, Hodder and Stoughton, 1971; Penguin, 1975

Orwell, George, *The Collected Essays, Journalism and Letters of George Orwell: Volume I: An Age Like This 1920–1940*, ed. Sonia Orwell and Ian Angus, Secker and Warburg, 1968; Penguin, 1970a

— *The Collected Essays, Journalism and Letters of George Orwell: Volume II: My Country Right or Left 1940–1943*, ed. Sonia Orwell and Ian Angus, Secker and Warburg, 1968; Penguin, 1970b

Powell, Anthony, *To Keep the Ball Rolling: The Memoirs of Anthony Powell*, Penguin, 1983 (abridgement of the four volumes published by William Heinemann, 1976–82)

Rhodes, Anthony, *Sword of Bone*, Faber and Faber, 1942

Rogers, Lindsay, *Guerilla Surgeon*, William Collins, 1957

T[hompson], T. J. and T[hompson], E. P. (eds.), *There is a Spirit in Europe . . .: A Memoir of Frank Thompson*, Victor Gollancz, 1947

Waugh, Evelyn, *Robbery Under Law: The Mexican Object-Lesson*, Chapman and Hall, 1939

HISTORICAL AND OTHER WORKS

Addison, Paul, *The Road to 1945: British Politics and the Second World War*, Jonathan Cape, 1975; Quartet, 1977

Brickhill, Paul, *The Great Escape*, Faber and Faber, 1951; Arrow, 1979

— *The Dam Busters*, Evans, 1951; Pan, 1954

Calder, Angus, *The People's War: Britain 1939–1945*, Jonathan Cape, 1969; Panther, 1972

Campbell, Christy, *World War II Fact Book*, Macdonald, 1985

Costello, John, *Love, Sex and War: Changing Values 1939–45*, William Collins, 1985; Pan, 1986

Harman, Nicholas, *Dunkirk: The Necessary Myth*, Hodder and Stoughton, 1980

Hastings, Max, *Overlord: D-Day and the Battle for Normandy*, Michael Joseph, 1984

Hewison, Robert, *Under Siege: Literary Life in London 1939–1945*, Weidenfeld and Nicolson, 1977

Lewis, Peter, *A People's War*, Thames Methuen, 1986

Marwick, Arthur, *The Home Front: The British and the Second World War*, Thames and Hudson, 1976

– *War and Social Change in the Twentieth Century*, Macmillan, 1974

Ryan, Cornelius, *The Longest Day*, Victor Gollancz, 1960

Sykes, Christopher, *Evelyn Waugh: A Biography*, William Collins, 1975; Penguin, 1977

Wintringham, Tom, *New Ways of War*, Penguin, 1940

CRITICISM

Comfort, Alex, *The Novel and Our Time*, Phoenix House, 1948

Harrisson, Tom, 'War Books', *Horizon* IV, 24 (December 1941), 416–37

Kermode, Frank, *The Sense of an Ending*, Oxford, 1969

Klein, Holger, 'Britain' in *The Second World War in Fiction*, ed. Holger Klein with John Flower and Eric Homberger, Macmillan, 1984

Lodge, David, *Working With Structuralism*, Routledge and Kegan Paul, 1981

Rutherford, Andrew, *The Literature of War: Five Studies in Heroic Virtue*, Macmillan, 1978

Spender, Stephen, *Life and the Poet*, Secker and Warburg, 1942

Sutherland, John, *Bestsellers: Popular Fiction of the 1970s*, Routledge and Kegan Paul, 1981

Tucker, James, *The Novels of Anthony Powell*, Macmillan, 1976

Worpole, Ken, *Dockers and Detectives: Popular Reading, Popular Writing*, Verso, 1983

Index